8501 EN
Addie's Long Summer

Lawlor, Laurie
ATOS BL 4.0
Points: 5.0

ADDIE'S LONG SUMMER

ADDIE'S
LONG SUMMER

Laurie Lawlor

Illustrated by Toby Gowing

Albert Whitman & Company

Morton Grove, Illinois

Also by Laurie Lawlor
Addie Across the Prairie
Addie's Dakota Winter
Daniel Boone
How to Survive Third Grade
Second-Grade Dog

"Sabula Song," on pages 51 and 52, was written by Miss French, a Sabula high school teacher. It appears in *Sabula, Iowa's Only Island City: 1835-1985,* Krabbenhoft Public Library, Sabula, Iowa, 1985.

"Starving to Death on a Government Claim," on page 76, is reprinted from *A Treasury of Nebraska Pioneer Folklore,* compiled by Roger L. Welsch, by permission of University of Nebraska Press. Copyright 1966 by the University of Nebraska Press.

Library of Congress Cataloging-in-Publication Data

Lawlor, Laurie.
    Addie's long summer/Laurie Lawlor;
illustrated by Toby Gowing.
      p. cm.
    Summary: Twelve-year-old Addie eagerly
awaits her cousins' summer visit to her prairie home but, once
they arrive, finds things much more complicated than she ever
imagined.
    ISBN 0-8075-0167-0
    [1. Cousins—Fiction. 2. Great Plains—Fiction. 3. Friend-
ship—Fiction.]
I. Gowing, Toby, ill. II. Title.
PZ7.L4189Aj 1992   91-34877
[Fic]—dc20   CIP
                                     AC

Text ©1992 by Laurie Lawlor.
Illustrations ©1992 by Toby Gowing.
Published in 1992 by Albert Whitman & Company,
6340 Oakton St., Morton Grove, Illinois 60053-2723.
Published simultaneously in Canada
by General Publishing, Limited, Toronto.
All rights reserved. Printed in the U.S.A.
10 9 8 7 6 5 4 3 2 1

WITHDRAWN

CONTENTS

For my grandfather, Rudolph Christian Trautman,
who dove the bluffs and swam the wide Missouri. L.L.

1 COUSINS COMING!

The red, unblinking eye of the sun peered over the horizon. Another scorcher on the way, and still no sign of rain. Twelve-year-old Addie wiped the sweat from her forehead. She tipped a heavy bucket under the third cottonwood sapling and watched the thirsty ground soak up the precious water.

When she stood up, she was nearly twice as tall as the four scrawny twigs Pa had so carefully planted beside the soddy. "Come October," he'd boasted, "Mother's shade trees will be as big as you."

Come October.

Addie took a deep breath. She did not want to think about October. Not today. Not when it was only June and she could concentrate on something else. Something agreeable. A visit from cousins who were coming all the way from Iowa! By evening, Pa would arrive in the wagon with Elizabeth and Maudie Nichols, the Mills family's very first visitors from Sabula.

Cousins—even the word sounded cozy and familiar. Addie swung the empty bucket and padded barefoot back to the pump.

Was it only a week ago that her family had received the letter from Aunt Rachel? How Mother's hand had trembled when she opened the pale blue envelope with the Iowa postmark! "Your sister and brother-in-law?" Pa's voice smacked the air like a firecracker on the Fourth of July. "Now those are the last two people I'd ever expect to hear from!"

Mother ignored Pa's remark and read aloud, "'Elizabeth has just turned twelve. Maudie is seventeen. They are quite capable, grown-up young ladies and should have no difficulty traveling on their own. We'll expect Samuel to meet them at the Defiance depot when the Chicago, Milwaukee, and Northwestern arrives at noon on Friday, June second.'"

A cousin exactly her age coming to Oak Hollow! Addie leaned all her eighty pounds on the squeaking pump handle, closed her eyes, and tried to conjure up memories. But the image of gawky, dark-haired Elizabeth shimmered and disappeared, like the illusion of distant water. Three years had passed since Addie's family left Iowa and journeyed by covered wagon to the Dakota Territory to homestead. Elizabeth had undoubtedly changed. After all, she was now "capable and grown-up."

Addie imagined a pretty, elegant cousin stepping from the wagon in a grey poplin frock with large magenta spots and a matching velvet sash—the most beautiful dress Addie had ever read about in the Montgomery Ward Catalog. Mother often said that no expense was too great for Aunt Rachel's girls. Elizabeth and Maudie had private lessons in French. They were learning to play the piano and to paint with fancy watercolors. All these were talents expected of young ladies who had "no difficulty traveling on their own."

Addie stopped pumping. What would Elizabeth think of *her?* Was she capable and grown-up? Could she ever leave home on her own? She peered at her blurred reflection in the soddy window. Would anyone ever call her pretty and poised? She brushed her hair away from her face. Her nose—wasn't it rather pointed? And her forehead was much too high. The dark eyes and full lips were nothing special. As for her hair, well, it was too straight, too brown, too dull—

"Addie! Vat's de matter vit you?"

Addie jumped at the sound of her friend's voice. "Nothing, Tilla," she said, trying to keep from blushing. "You just surprised me, that's all."

Tilla pouted, her hands on her hips. "You forget tutoring is today, Miss Teacher?"

9

Addie shook her head. "I didn't forget. But why are you here so early?"

"Papa says I can only stay until ten for our reading lesson." Tilla grinned. One scruffy blonde braid was nearly undone. Dust from the five-mile walk from Ree Heights clung to her lean neck and around her thin lips. "You bet I leaf quick before he change his mind. Say, you can't put no more vater in dat bucket."

"*Any* more water."

"Any more vater." Tilla's hands fluttered as if to brush away the stubborn English words. "Vant some help?"

Together the girls hauled the bucket and finished watering the last sapling.

"Hello, Tilla!" Mother called. She came around the corner of the house carrying a bouquet of golden alexander, deep orange Indian paint, and pale purple prairie phlox. The wind billowed her worn, white apron. Sunlight glinted against her steel shears.

"Good morning, Mrs. Mills." Tilla hungrily sniffed the lingering aroma of freshly baked sponge cake. "You cooking someting special today?"

"Company's coming," Mother replied.

"Company?"

"Please, let me tell her, Mother," Addie begged. "You'll never guess, Tilla. We must have written a hundred letters inviting our relatives to visit. And now, at last, cousins

10

are coming from Iowa—today! Mother's turned the house topsy-turvy getting ready."

Mother cocked her head. "Aren't you exaggerating just a bit?"

Addie shook her head. Since the arrival of Aunt Rachel's letter, the whole family had been busy cleaning every nook and cranny of the soddy. Pa recovered the walls with fresh, clean newspaper. Eleven-year-old George and seven-year-old Lew scrubbed the rough, pine-board floor with soap and water and polished all the forks and knives with stove ashes. Burt, who was five, and Nellie May, who was three, helped re-stuff mattresses with new dry corncobs. Addie sewed a curtain for the soddy's only window using the end of a bolt of red gingham. To hide the canned goods, Mother made little skirts for the shelves. The house had never looked better.

Tilla scratched her neck. "How far is Iova?"

"Nearly sixteen hours on the train," Mother said.

"How many cousins?"

"Two girls," Addie replied eagerly. "Elizabeth and Maudie. Elizabeth is exactly my age."

Tilla arched an eyebrow. "I haf cousins who come from Norvay last year. Dey are still at our house. Are dese cousins coming to live vit you forever?"

"They won't be here forever, certainly," Mother said. "They have their own family back in Sabula. And of course they'll need to be back at school in the fall."

Addie frowned. "But exactly how long will the cousins be visiting, Mother? I hope it's not just a very short time."

"I don't know exactly how long they'll be with us. But I'm sure Aunt Rachel will write and tell us when it's time for them to go home."

"So dey vill not stay forever, huh?" Tilla crossed her wiry arms in front of herself in a satisfied way that Addie found vaguely annoying. "And your flowers, are dey for da Iova cousins?"

Mother nodded. "Pretty, aren't they? Even in this dry, hot weather, some flowers are still thriving. And how are you doing in this heat, Tilla? How is your family?"

"Not so good. Our house is very hot, very crowded. Clara's babies vill come very soon, and my sister is suspecting in August. I tink it vill be a big batch dis time because she is very fat. How vill ve get rid of so many?"

"You think your sister is expecting twins? Surely you don't mean you'll give her babies away?"

"No, ve must get rid of puppies. Clara is our big black dog." Tilla sighed. "My sister's baby, I suppose ve vill haf to keep dat one like all de oders. I don't like all de babies. I don't want to stay home no more and take care of dem. One baby comes, den anoder. Den anoder. I never get to go back to school."

Tilla's scowl prompted Addie to change the subject. "That sponge cake smells so good, Mother. When will we eat?"

"As soon as your father and the cousins arrive."

"Vat else you having?" Tilla asked.

"Beefsteak, mashed potatoes, spiced watermelon-rind pickles, corn relish, fresh baking soda biscuits, and the first green peas and radishes from the garden," Mother said.

"And?" Addie demanded.

"And what?"

"Haven't you forgotten something?"

"Seems like plenty to me."

"Mother," Addie insisted, "don't you remember what you promised?"

"Oh, yes. Of course. The canned peaches."

Addie smiled. For months, she and her brothers and sister had been waiting to taste the store-bought fruit that stood with such solemn mystery on the back of the root cellar shelf. Now at last they would have their chance.

Snip! Snip! Mother trimmed the flower stems. "I was just thinking, Addie, when we get word that you've won that scholarship to high school, we'll have an even bigger feast. You'll come, too, won't you, Tilla? And we'll invite your teacher, Miss Brophy. And our dear neighbors, the Fencys. Won't that be lovely?"

Addie's smile vanished. Why did Mother have to bring up high school and ruin everything?

Happily, Tilla clapped. "Vill ve haf canned peaches, too?"

Mother laughed. "Of course. Why not? It's not every day that we have such a wonderful reason to celebrate. In a few years Addie is going to be the very first Mills to graduate from high school. And she'll have a teaching certificate, too."

Addie tried to smile. She was supposed to be a happy, grateful scholar, one of only three students in all of Hutchinson County invited to compete for the scholarship to high school in Yankton. "The test is not until August— that's a long way off, Mother," she said. "Nearly three months. And school doesn't start until October. What if I don't get the highest score?"

"Of course you'll get the highest score. Why, just the other day Miss Brophy told me that she couldn't think of anyone better qualified to win that scholarship than you." Beaming, Mother turned to Tilla. "I just have to tell everyone the good news. Mr. Mills and I are so proud of Addie. She is going to be the very first teacher in our family."

Addie's shoulders sagged. She did not feel the least bit confident.

"Ya, Addie is sure lucky," Tilla said slowly.

Addie avoided her friend's eyes. Why did Mother and Pa have to embarrass her by bragging in front of other people all the time? She was sick to death of hearing about how proud they were. "Mother? Can Tilla and I go down to Rattling Creek to start her lesson? I found a new story in the newspaper she might like."

"A new story!" Tilla exclaimed. "Oh, please yes! I hope it's better dan 'Charlotte Temple's Shame.' 'Alas! My torn heart!' Den dat helpless Charlotte faints in de arms of her betrayer. Vat a fool! If I vas dat Charlotte, I give dat Montraville a good vop in de head! If she vant dis scoundrel so bad, she should send her broders after him. Dat's all. Den Montraville marries her or dey kill him."

Mother looked alarmed. "I thought you were using the *McGuffey Reader*—"

"Oh, no!" Tilla interrupted. "Romances are much better."

"And Tilla is making great progress," Addie said, hoping she sounded as authoritative as a real schoolteacher.

Mother frowned. "It just doesn't seem quite proper. What's wrong with reading some nice Bible stories?"

Addie had to think fast. "We also practice reading the news. Why don't you let us shell peas for you while we have our lesson?" Before Mother could answer, Addie hurried inside the house. She grabbed the bowl of peas

15

from the table and found the newspaper.

The girls giggled as they escaped down the path that led to a secluded spot where the creek made a slight bend. Box elders and cottonwoods arched over the water and shut out the big sky. The current chuckled over worn, round rocks. In the sandy flats, the creek riffled and whispered. Near the big, gnarled roots of trees, the water was deepest and darkest, and it didn't move at all.

A killdeer hidden among the pungent wolf willows noisily called his name, "Kill-deah! Kill-deah! Dee-dee-dee." Tilla paused, as if to soak in all the green mysterious scents and sounds. "See here vat I brought you, Miss Teacher!" From her apron pocket she took something wrapped in a soiled handkerchief.

Addie gingerly undid the smelly bundle. Not that strange Norwegian goat cheese again! "Why thank you, Tilla," she said with as much enthusiasm as she could muster. She had never gotten used to Tilla's foreign-tasting food. This time she had also brought along thin, brittle flatbread and a slice of dried fish, fragile as old paper. Addie felt guilty accepting Tilla's gifts, which surely depleted her family's meager larder. "You know you don't have to bring something every time you come for our lessons."

"I know. I vant to. Dat's vy I do it. You are my very best friend in de whole vorld. And dis is our very own magic place dat nobody knows but us. Am I right?"

Addie nodded. This bend in Rattling Creek was their own private, enchanted world. Here, she and Tilla pretended they lived in a palace or commanded a pirate ship. As long as Pa or Mother didn't call her away to finish some chore, or her brothers and sister didn't interrupt, she and Tilla could transform this spot into anything they wished. An orphanage. A jungle camp. A haunted house. A mountain hideout. A battlefield. A deserted island in the middle of the ocean.

Addie sat down, the bowl of peas at her side, the newspaper in her lap.

Tilla leaned back in the grass. "I got to tell you someting on my mind because you are my friend. It seems to me you don't seem so happy no more about going avay."

"*Any* more."

Tilla groaned impatiently. "You know vat I mean. Remember ven you first hear about dis scholarship? You vas so excited. You tell me, 'Tilla, now I get a chance to be somebody.' You talk about how you vas going to teach and write poems in your spare time and be famous—"

"I don't want to discuss it." Addie pursed her lips. She flipped through the *Dakota Citizen* for May 20, 1886.

"Look at you. All frowns. Vy? Are you scared now October is closer? Or maybe you vorry about dat test."

Addie shrugged as if she did not really care. But deep down, she did.

17

Deep down, she was terrified. What if she failed? What would her parents and Miss Brophy think of her then?

"Papa tells me Yankton is forty American miles from here. Is dat vat makes you vorry? You be homesick in a big city far from your folks?"

"I said I don't want to talk about it."

Tilla laced her fingers behind her head and stubbornly waited. Minutes ticked by. Finally, unable to bear the silence any longer, Addie picked up a rock and hurled it into the water. "You don't understand. Everything is already arranged. Miss Brophy has found a family in town who says I can live in their house and eat their food if I take care of their children. My room and board will be free. But I don't even know these people. I'll be living all by myself in a new place with strangers."

"And your schooling, it vill be free, too?"

"If I get a high enough score on the test, I'll get the scholarship. But don't you see? Yankton is a big city with lots of people, and nobody knows me. What if everyone is unfriendly? What will it be like to have to live in a place like that when I can't come home except on holidays?"

"You get your own room?"

"Yes, in their attic."

"And you don't haf to vatch dose children all de time, do you?"

"Not when I have to go to school or study."

"And do you haf to do laundry or clean or cook?"

Addie shook her head.

Tilla whistled between her teeth. "Sounds very good. If I vas you, I could hardly vait."

Addie fumed. What did Tilla know? She had never lived on her own. She didn't know the first thing about the dangers of big cities—getting lost or robbed or trampled by runaway teams and wagons.

If it were only possible to stop time! Then there would be nothing to decide—whether to stay or to go. October would never come, and her life would continue just as it always had. Her secret would be safe.

"Don't be angry, Addie," Tilla said. "Maybe I could take dat test, too. Maybe next year ven I catch up. Den ve go to school in Yankton together, and you don't be so lonely."

Addie squirmed. Tilla had such big, impossible dreams. Of all the students at Hutchinson County School, she had had the most promise. She was Miss Brophy's shining star until her mother died two years ago. That was when her father made her quit school and stay home to take care of the house and her younger sister. And now she had to help with her older sisters' babies, too.

"I vish I vas you so I take dat test and git out of here," Tilla said softly.

Addie did not look at Tilla. She felt too ashamed.

"I git my own place to live in da city," Tilla continued. "I git a job vere I do vat I like. I take my clothes to de laundry. I eat out of cans. I lif like lady and I never marry anyone."

"Never marry? Why?" Addie asked, surprised. In all the romances they had read together, the women who lived happily ever after always married handsome, rich men.

"If I don't marry, I don't haf to answer to no husband. If I move far avay, I don't haf to answer to no fader, no broder either." Tilla spit out a piece of grass. "You know vat your problem is, Addie? You haf no problem. All you haf is good luck."

"You don't know what you're talking about."

"I do. I know plenty. How come you so afraid? Sometime I tink you are getting as stupid as dat stupid Charlotte in de story."

Addie stood up so quickly that she knocked over the bowl of peas. "I think our lesson for today is cancelled."

Tilla stood up, too. She lifted her determined jaw and clenched her fists the way she did when she was ready to argue. But she did not speak another word. She simply slipped through the willows and disappeared.

Tilla, outspoken Tilla, was gone. Instead of relief, Addie felt only sadness. Now there was no one to whom she could tell her awful secret.

She had not mailed the signed document to the Yankton Board of Examiners, the document that said she would take that scholarship test. The deadline for filing the application was August 1, only two months away. Yet the letter, complete with postage, remained hidden along with her most precious belongings, inside a wooden cigar box in the barn.

Addie sighed and bent over to scoop up the spilled peas. The motionless air along the creek suddenly felt stifling. There seemed to be nowhere to escape from the heat or from the shame of her own lie.

2 DRESSED AND DIRTY

Late that afternoon, lightning flickered on the horizon. High, heavy clouds gathered, covering the sun. Addie and her brothers watched and waited. Nobody spoke. Maybe this time it would rain. A corkscrew of grit danced across the yard. Then, like some ill-tempered trickster, the wind pushed the thunderheads to some other farm in some other part of the territory, and the sun shone down again as relentlessly as before.

The children went back to the hateful chore of cleaning the privy. George and Burt practiced making explosive toots between their pressed palms. Passing Dakota wind, they called it. They thought they were very funny. Addie was disgusted. What would refined young ladies like her cousins think of such behavior?

Addie pumped a bucket of water, added lye, and handed Burt and Lew two old brooms for scrubbing the privy floor. Her job was to scour the wooden seat of the two-holer with a brush. Today the worst chore was George's. "It's your turn to sprinkle lime powder into the pit," she announced.

"The abominable pit, you mean. Kind of reminds me of that sinkhole out near the creek. Fall in there and you'll suffocate just as fast." George wrinkled up his nose and leafed through the outhouse reading material, a two-year-old Montgomery Ward catalog. "You hear the joke about the man who got caught in the dust storm?"

"Stop joshing and get to work," Addie ordered. "You're just stalling."

"Go ahead and tell it," Burt said encouragingly. He liked George's jokes, especially ones that involved guts or other unmentionable body parts.

George grinned. "See, there's this farmer's wife, and she's walking to the barn after a bad dust blizzard. Dirt is piled up thick as snow. She spots a doorknob in a hill of dust, pulls it, and there's a man with his overalls down. 'Good morning, sir,' she says. 'Has the storm blown off your clothes?' And the man replies, 'No, ma'am, and I'll thank you to close the outhouse door.'" George slapped Burt on the back. The two of them laughed and laughed. Lew grinned.

"Ha, ha. Very funny," Addie replied. "But you still haven't done your job yet, George."

George made a little bow. He picked up the box of

lime and dashed bravely into the outhouse. In less than a minute, he staggered outside, gasping dramatically for air.

"Think fast, Lew!" Burt grabbed the empty bucket and hurled it at his brother. As usual, Lew didn't make the catch. The bucket clanked and tumbled on the ground.

"Burt, why do you always have to do that?" Addie demanded.

"Yeah, you know Lew can't catch," George added.

Addie handed the bucket to Lew. His knuckles went white as he clutched the handle. Addie wondered why George and Burt couldn't leave Lew alone. Was it his fault if he was clumsy? It wasn't fair. They knew he wouldn't fight back. He always said he preferred to talk his way out of actual combat because he got nosebleeds so easily. But the real reason he wouldn't even defend himself, Addie knew, was that he couldn't stomach the violence. "It makes me sick," he once confided to her. "What's the point of getting punched and trying to punch back, just to make the other fellow sorry?"

"Let's finish this privy as fast as we can, all right?" Addie said to divert her brothers' attention. "Mother said the cousins could be here in less than an hour."

George gazed at his sister as if she were crazy. "Cousins! I am sick and tired of hearing about cousins!"

"What's so great about cousins coming?" Burt agreed.

"Especially *girl* cousins."

"Well, I can think of one good thing," Lew piped up. "You and me and George get to camp out in the barn loft. That will be fun."

Burt and George nodded. "We can stay up as late as we want," Burt said eagerly.

"Pa and Mother will never know," George added. "Why, I might even teach you boys how to smoke a piece of clothesline rope."

"George Sydney Mills!" Addie threatened. "Don't you dare say one more word!" How many times had Pa warned them about the hazards of starting a fire in the brand-new barn?

"Say," Burt interrupted, "when we're finished here, why don't we scout around for that murdering, runaway stagecoach robber? I heard there's a thousand-dollar reward. We could split it four ways and be rich."

"Where do you get such crazy ideas?" Addie demanded. Last week she had overheard Mr. Fency warning Pa that a prisoner had escaped from two U.S. deputy marshals on the train to Running Water. Immediately, she had imagined a runaway outlaw as cold-blooded and wily as Billy the Kid. Although the Kid had been gunned down by the law in 1881, almost five years ago, authentic accounts of his life story appeared regularly in the *Dakota Citizen* and kept his legend very much alive.

"Rumor is that the outlaw's a crazy fellow," Lew said in a low voice. "They say he's got an awful temper."

"An awful temper?" Addie gulped. What if the escaped prisoner, disguised by a black slouch hat, was hiding in their cornfield?

"And he's so strong that it took six men to lock him up," Burt added. "His chest is as round as a tree trunk. He has a bull neck, black shaggy hair, and a moustache like a hat rack. He's a dead shot with a six-shooter. And right before he jumped off that moving train, he knocked the deputies' heads together. Killed them instantly."

Addie's eyes narrowed. "Who told you all this?"

"George. Ask him."

George whistled softly and dug his big toe into the dirt.

"Go on, George. Show her," Lew hissed.

George stuffed his hand into his pocket. "All right. Only don't let Mother know. I took this from the Defiance livery wall and she might get mad." He held out a wadded yellow paper.

Addie smoothed the poster and read:

Read and Reflect!
Murders and high-handed outrages have been of such frequent occurrence as to excite the just indignation of all good citizens of Defiance. CRIME

MUST AND WILL BE SUPPRESSED. All offenders will be summarily dealt with and punished by HANGING FROM THE NECK. One-thousand-dollar reward for any information leading to the capture and arrest of the masked bandit who robbed the stage to Larimore, killed the driver, and escaped from U. S. Marshal custody on May 15, 1886. He is considered dangerous.

— The Defiance Vigilance Committee

"See?" Burt said proudly. "We weren't making it up."

"I still say it's a lot of foolishness," Addie said. But she could not shrug off a new worry. What if the outlaw was lurking along the road from Defiance? What if he ambushed Pa and the cousins? She frowned.

"We're going to track him down," Burt said, "and divide up the reward. I'm going to buy a fast saddle horse and my own hunting dog. Lew's going to buy a set of books that have fancy leather covers with gold letters, and George is going to buy—"

"George is going to buy nothing!" Addie snapped. "George, what do you think you're doing, filling their heads with all this nonsense? You can't go snooping around after outlaws. Outlaws are dangerous."

George spat defiantly on the ground. "You're no fun,

Addie. What's wrong with dreaming about being rich and famous?"

"Addie!" Mother's voice rang out. "George, Burt, and Lew! Come inside now and get cleaned up. Then I want you to keep an eye on Nellie May so I can finish getting the cousins' beds ready."

Addie gave George a threatening look before they went inside. As soon as Nellie May, Addie, and the boys were properly washed up and dressed in their best Sunday clothes, they sauntered to the corral in front of the barn.

The barn, which had been built earlier that spring, was one of the largest in the county. The foundation was constructed of stone, and the walls were made of expensive timber, shipped all the way from Wisconsin. There were two large doors at each end. As soon as the barn was finished, a new root cellar was dug several yards from the soddy.

Pa never did anything haphazardly. Nicknamed "Doc Mills" by neighbors who came to see him for livestock advice, Pa was respected for his know-how and his attention to detail. He had planned and overseen the construction crew from start to finish. George had worked long and hard on the project. And if something wasn't right, Pa made him or the other workers do it over— no mistakes were allowed.

Addie, who was the only one wearing shoes, perched

with her sullen brothers on the gate. She smoothed the front of her starched, white apron and wiggled her toes inside her uncomfortable leather boots. "Remember what Mother said," she reminded her brothers. "No fighting. No getting dirty. No coming inside the house again until supper's ready."

The boys groaned. Nellie May plopped herself in the dirt and began poking pebbles between her toes.

"Nellie! Get off the ground! What do you think you're doing?"

"Leave us alone! Me and McCoggy are busy."

Addie rolled her eyes. McCoggy was Nellie's invisible friend. The most Nellie would ever tell anyone about McCoggy was that he was as fat as a ripe watermelon and enjoyed being naughty. "You and McCoggy get off the ground right this minute."

"No. We're making new toes."

The boys hooted.

"I'm going to count to ten and you better—" Addie threatened.

Nellie jumped to her feet and smiled coyly at her brothers. Suddenly, she lifted her starched gingham dress over her head so that her white drawers showed. Her brothers burst into loud laughter.

"There goes Nellie Half-Naked!" Burt howled.

"Put your dress down, Nellie!" Addie ordered. "And

don't you dare use that word, Burt."

"What word?"

"You know what word I mean."

"What's wrong with *naked?*"

"Yeah," George snickered, "it sounds all right to me."

"It's not...civilized," Addie said in exasperation. How would she ever manage to control this mob and make a good impression on the cousins?

While Burt mouthed "naked, naked, naked," George rolled up the sleeves of his clean, pressed shirt. "What do you want to do now, George?" Lew asked.

"I dunno," George replied. "What do you want to do, Burt?"

"I dunno," Burt said, and grinned. "What do you want to do, Nellie Half-Naked?"

Right on cue, Nellie hoisted her dress over her head again.

"Stop it!" Addie shook her finger at her sister. "Don't you know proper ladies don't do that, Nellie?"

Burt belched approvingly. "Nellie's no lady!"

"Nellie's no lady!" Nellie repeated. She climbed up on the gate and sat beside her brothers, careful to leave plenty of space for McCoggy.

"I'm bored," Lew complained.

George sniffed the air. "I'm hungry. Do you think Mother would give me a couple of those biscuits?"

Addie shook her head. "The biscuits are for the cousins. Can't you think of something else to do besides eat?"

"I know!" George announced. He whispered something to Lew. The two boys disappeared inside the barn. What were they up to now?

In a few minutes, George returned. He raced around, waving his arms to clear away squawking chickens from the barn doorway. His cap was turned backward and a hen feather was stuck rakishly in the brim. "Stand back! Stand back!" he shouted. "Give the performers some room!"

Burt applauded. Addie craned her neck for a better look. Maybe one of George's shows would help pass the time. At least it was more constructive than stealing biscuits or teasing Nellie May. "Nellie, keep still or you'll fall on your head," Addie warned. But Nellie wouldn't listen. Excitedly, she bounced up and down.

George put his fist to his mouth and made a sound like a horn. "Here he comes now, ladies and gentlemen. The one, the only—Miry the Magnificent!"

From the shadows of the barn charged Miry, the year-old pig. Hanging onto his back for dear life was Lew, who waved a fishing pole with a dried ear of corn tied to the end of the line. The corn dangled just out of Miry's reach.

"Stop it!" Addie jumped down from the gate. "You're

31

going to get all dirty riding that pig!"

Lew paid no attention. Miry slowed to a walk on his second time around the barnyard.

"You're a charmer, aren't you, Miry?" Lew gave the pig a quick scratch behind his bristly ears. Miry wheezed like an old bagpipe.

"What's he saying?" Burt asked, grinning.

"He says, 'Thank you very much,'" Lew translated. "Isn't Miry the smartest, handsomest pig you've ever seen?"

"Just remember, Miry," George warned, "stay out of the cream."

"Last time Pa caught Miry in the cream, remember what he said?" Burt reminded them. "'I don't like this pig's eating habits. He's getting too big for a pet.'"

Addie glanced at Lew. "Shut up, Burt. We all heard what Pa said. Come on, now. The show's over. Get off before Mother sees you."

Miry came to a halt as soon as Lew lifted the ear of corn out of sight. Lew climbed off and gave Miry a pat. He sprinkled a pocketful of corn on the ground. Miry ate greedily.

"Addie?" Lew asked softly, while George and Burt were busy poking each other with the fishing pole, "you don't think Pa's going to get rid of Miry, do you?"

Addie sighed. Why couldn't Lew accept the fact that animals on the farm weren't pets? One day, Miry would be sold and sent away like the other hogs. But she didn't say this to her troubled brother. Instead, she tousled his fuzzy blond hair. "Don't worry so much, Lew. Come on and brush yourself off."

Miry was unofficially Lew's pig. When Miry's mother had died, Lew was the one who insisted on feeding the runt. Miry lapped cow's milk from Lew's fingers. Eventually, the pig learned to lap up milk from a bowl like a cat. He grew to a weight of nearly three hundred pounds. Miry was privileged. While the other pigs were penned up, he was allowed to accompany the children on chores or on trips to the creek.

Burt grabbed the pole from George and leapt onto Miry's back. "Look at me! I'm a rip-roaring desperado!" he shouted. Miry began trotting as soon as he saw the bobbing corn again. But no matter how fast he moved, he could not reach the tasty snack.

"*My* turn!" Nellie demanded. "Then McCoggy. McCoggy wants a ride, too."

"You and McCoggy are too little." Addie grabbed her sister out of the way as Miry stampeded past.

"McCoggy's big. I'm big, too!"

"You don't want to get all dirty like those disgusting boys, do you, Nellie? Somebody has to be nice and clean when the cousins come."

"I hate this dress! I hate you! Me and McCoggy want

33

a ride! Give us a ride!"

Addie shook her head. Why did things like this always have to happen at the worst possible moment?

"Watch me, George!" Burt cried. "I'm galloping to catch the stagecoach!" The closer he held the dangling ear of corn to Miry's snout, the faster the pig went.

"Ya-hoo!" George yodeled. "Here comes Billy the Kid!"

"Burt, you've got to stop!" Addie commanded. "Look at you! Your face is all grimy. And what's Mother going to say when she sees you riding a pig in your good clothes?"

"I don't know and I don't care! I'm a gun-slinging sharpshooter with a price on my head! Yip-ee-yi! Yip-ee-yo!" Burt gave Miry a nudge with his heels. The pig took off like a shot. Still gripping the pole, Burt dove for Miry's neck. Miry zoomed out of the barnyard. The corncob waved violently in front of him as he galloped faster and faster, through the gate and around the barn twice.

"Help!" shouted Burt as he came around the second time. No longer the proud outlaw, he had slipped off to one side and was being dragged through the dirt in a humiliating fashion.

"Drop the pole!" George hollered.

Burt was too panic-stricken to follow this suggestion. He held tight to the bobbing stick and the pig's neck. Miry headed straight for the manure pile. With a thump,

Burt tumbled in. He sat up, unhurt but covered with dung. Miry squeaked and made a quick lunge. The corn was his at last! He scampered behind the barn to eat his treasure.

Burt's best shirt was ripped. His face and hair and clothes were smeared with manure. "George Sidney Mills! Lewis Warren Mills! It's not funny!" Addie screamed. "Get up and stop howling and rolling around. You're both only getting dirtier."

But it was too late.

Beyond the next rise, she spotted Pa and the wagon. Seated beside Pa were two figures concealed beneath parasols.

The cousins!

3 MAUDIE AND ELIZABETH

Addie raced to the pump and filled an empty bucket with water. "Take this to the barn, George! And make sure Lew and Burt scrub themselves. There's not much we can do about the smell. Nellie, you come with me."

"No, McCoggy doesn't want to!" Nellie whined, both feet planted firmly on the ground.

Addie picked up Nellie under one arm and galloped toward the soddy. "Mother!" she shouted. "I can see Pa. The cousins are coming!"

Mother hurried outside, untying her apron. "What's wrong with Nellie? And why is her dress dirty, Addie? I thought I told you to keep your eye on the children. Here, Nellie, you come inside with me."

There was no time to explain what had really happened. Addie sighed. She watched the parasols coming closer.

"Whoa!" Pa shouted, pulling the horses to a halt beside the barn. "Becca? Our company's come!"

Addie's hands shook as she tried to tidy her hair. What was that shuffling sound behind her? She spun around.

George, Lew, and Burt swaggered through the dust, twirling invisible six-shooters. They grinned at Addie and punched each other. They'd hardly washed at all. The dirty streaks on their faces made them look like masked bandits.

"Don't you dare say one rude thing to Maudie and Elizabeth," she threatened her brothers in a low voice.

"Yes, sir!" George made a mock salute. Burt and Lew did the same.

"Children, come over here and say hello," Pa called. He took one look at the boys and frowned. "What happened to you? I was hoping you'd have sense enough to stay clean until your cousins arrived."

Addie took a hesitant step toward the parasols. "Hello, Maudie. Hello, Elizabeth."

The parasol that was the color of an overripe plum twirled dramatically. Two shrewd, black eyes peered down at Addie. "I'm Elizabeth. She's Maudie," announced a clear voice. The parasol snapped shut.

Elizabeth's pale, heart-shaped face and dark hair were framed by a large, white sailor hat with blue ribbon streamers down the back. She wore a dainty, white sailor dress with long sleeves and a full pleated skirt. Her collar and cuffs were edged with blue trim that matched the

37

buttons on the front of her dress. A blue sailor's kerchief was neatly tied around her neck, and on her hands were spotless white kid gloves. Addie wondered how those gloves had managed to stay so clean during the long, dusty trip.

Elizabeth flashed a charming smile. "Hello, Addie— my Dakota cousin. It's been such a long time, hasn't it? Mother says you have become a great reader, so I brought you some books."

Addie blushed with pleasure. Books! What a thoughtful present. Elizabeth must like to read, too. Suddenly she was certain that she and her cousin would become the very best of friends.

Elizabeth leapt from the wagon without snagging her fashionable bustle. Expertly, she adjusted the gathered material at the back of her skirt. "And you must be George and Burt and Lew." She shook a dirty paw of each smelly boy, as if he were quite clean and proper and grown-up. George whistled under his breath, the way he did when he was impressed.

"Maudie, say hello to your Dakota cousins!" Elizabeth ordered.

The black parasol shuddered and collapsed. Maudie was a plain, brown wren of a girl. It did not seem possible that she could be the older sister of someone as sophisticated and winsome as Elizabeth. She was shapelessly plump, and her complexion was as pallid as pie dough. Her eyes

were the color of dirty ice. She folded and unfolded her large, ungainly hands. "Pleased to meet you," she mumbled. As she struggled with the clasp, the parasol slipped to the ground.

"Not again, Maudie! You must have dropped that at least a dozen times since we left Sabula," Elizabeth scolded. "If your head were not fastened securely on your neck, you'd probably lose that, too."

Burt and George snickered. Addie did not move. Maudie was seventeen. Would she let her younger sister talk to her that way?

"Sorry," was all Maudie said. But she continued to look down at the parasol. Was she hoping that it might somehow float back up by itself?

"Here, my dear," Mother murmured, hurrying toward the wagon. She handed Maudie her parasol. "Welcome to Oak Hollow."

"Aunty Becca!" Elizabeth exclaimed, and kissed Mother on the cheek. Maudie climbed out of the wagon. Like Elizabeth, she was wearing too many clothes for such hot weather. Although her hat was trimmed with feathers and her drop-waist dress was of expensive, green-striped taffeta, Maudie seemed as ordinary as if she were wearing an old sunbonnet and a plain flour-sack dress. She embraced Mother awkwardly and blushed.

"See here, Aunty Becca. I've brought presents for each

of my dear cousins." Elizabeth reached inside her smart traveling pouch and pulled out a paper sack filled with black licorice strips. George, Lew, and Burt cheered. Carefully, Elizabeth divided the candy among the Mills children. Addie smiled politely and tucked the licorice in her apron pocket. Her brothers, without even bothering to thank Elizabeth, immediately took huge chomps.

Burt spit on the ground. "Will you look at that?" he said. "Black licorice makes the same color spit as tobacco."

George winked at Addie and spit some licorice juice, too.

"That's enough, boys," Pa scolded. "Thank your cousin and eat your candy properly."

The boys dug their bare toes into the dirt, mumbled thanks, and kept gnawing with their mouths wide open, so everyone could plainly see their black teeth and tongues.

"It was very thoughtful of you to bring licorice, Elizabeth." Mother smiled fondly at her nieces.

"You have a delightful farm, Uncle Samuel. Look at that enormous barn! Much bigger than any others we saw along the way, don't you agree, Maudie?"

Maudie nodded and twisted her green taffeta dress sash. "Yes, it seems quite spacious," she said quietly.

Pa looked very pleased.

"How was your trip?" Mother asked.

"I thought we would never get here," Elizabeth said.

"What a wide open place! Why, have you noticed? There's nothing in Dakota to make a shadow!"

Addie smiled. "You get used to it after a while."

Elizabeth placed her hands on her hips. "You must have had remarkable courage to come out here and start homesteading."

"Anybody with a dream big enough can find plenty of space in Dakota," Pa said, grinning. "That's why they call it the Land of Begin Again."

"Did you hear that, Maudie? The Land of Begin Again. Isn't that wonderful?"

Maudie looked away, her face flushed.

"We got plenty of space. And we got plenty of coyotes and rattlesnakes, too," George said.

Elizabeth look startled. "You do?"

Addie gave her brother a kick. "George is only trying to spook you. Don't pay him any mind."

Elizabeth sniffed. "I don't scare that easily, I can assure you."

George grinned.

"Dakota does take a bit of getting used to. But I'm sure you'll have no trouble," Pa said, smiling. "George, you can help me carry in Maudie's and Elizabeth's trunks."

"Has anyone seen Nellie May?" Mother asked. "I thought she followed me outside."

"She and McCoggy are chasing Miry," Burt said.

42

"Who's McCoggy? Who's Miry?" Elizabeth asked. "More Dakota cousins?"

"McCoggy's invisible," Burt explained. "And Miry's not a cousin. He's a pig."

"Oh, I see," Elizabeth replied, flicking a burr from her sleeve.

"Nellie May! Where are you?" Mother called.

Waving a stick, Nellie ran from behind the barn. "Here, Miry! Give me a ride!" The three-hundred-pound pig bolted past her, wheezing wildly. He hurtled through the yard, crashed into the pump, fell over, and struggled to his feet. Then he dashed toward the cousins.

Maudie screamed. All the color drained from Elizabeth's face. The cousins scrambled back into the wagon. They opened and shut their parasols, as if to scare away the pig. "Don't worry!" Addie shouted as she waved her apron. "I'll keep him away from you."

George and Burt and Lew joined in the chase. They made several unsuccessful tackles. Finally, they gave up, out of breath. Miry wobbled and collapsed behind the privy. "What in the world is the matter with that pig?" Mother said, her face flushed. "He's usually so friendly."

"He seems very wild," Maudie whispered. "Does he bite?"

"No, I think he's just skunked. Somebody's been racing him too hard in this heat." Pa looked accusingly at George.

"Skunked?" Elizabeth repeated.

"He's tired out and a little crazy from the weather," Addie explained.

"We'll just let him be now. He'll recover in a little while. He's really perfectly harmless," Pa said. "George, help me with the trunks." George pulled the smallest trunk from the wagon and staggered toward the door.

"Elizabeth and Maudie, why don't you girls come inside? I'm sure you're both tired after your long trip," Mother said. "We'll have supper on the table in just a few minutes."

After looking cautiously all around, the cousins again climbed out of the wagon. Elizabeth hurried across the yard, right behind Mother. "Aunty Becca, is this the...the house?"

"Yes, it is," Mother said proudly.

Addie held her breath. What was her cousin thinking? What would she say?

With the end of her parasol, Elizabeth poked a crumbly sod brick. "My goodness! It *is* made of dirt!" she exclaimed in her ringing voice. And then, with only a slight hesitation, she added, "How utterly charming! There's a flower growing on the roof. Come along, Maudie."

4 NEURASTHENIA

"You going to finish that biscuit or just leave it sit there?" Burt asked Elizabeth at supper. The cousins had cut their beefsteak into tiny chunks with their black-handled knives, but they had not eaten one piece. They had nibbled and jabbed peas with their three-tined forks. The rest of the food on their tin plates was not even touched.

Wasted was what Pa usually would have called it.

But since the cousins were guests, neither Pa nor Mother made any comment.

"Don't be rude, Burton Grant. Maybe Elizabeth isn't hungry," Mother murmured. Her brow was wrinkled. Her smile seemed strained. Addie hated to see Mother looking so disappointed. Why weren't the cousins eating the food she had so carefully prepared?

"Just wait until you see what's for dessert!" Addie said. She hoped her cousins would feel just as excited as she did about real store-bought, canned peaches that had cost the remarkable sum of twenty cents.

"I haven't ate a peach since I don't know when. I could handle a couple bowls full!" George boasted.

"Me, too," Lew said dreamily.

"Me, three!" Nellie pounded the table with her spoon.

Mother carefully divided into nine bowls the slippery, glittering peaches swimming in sweet syrup. Addie held her bowl near her face. The aroma was as delicate and lovely as a blooming fruit tree.

"Here you go, Elizabeth and Maudie," Mother said, holding out a bowl to each niece.

"None for me, thank you," Elizabeth replied politely.

"Thank you, none for me," Maudie echoed.

"I suppose," Elizabeth explained, "Mother forgot to tell you that Maudie and I have delicate constitutions. We don't eat meat. We don't eat sugar. We prefer natural grains and breads made with Dr. Graham's special flour. By following this special diet, Mother says, we will avoid neurasthenia."

"Neurasthenia!" Pa thumped the table with his fist. "What in heaven's name is that?"

"It is a disease that is mostly absent from the countryside. Perhaps that's why you haven't heard of it." Elizabeth flashed a charming smile.

Pa's scowl remained unchanged. "Exactly what are the symptoms?"

"Skin rash, headache, hysteria, brain-collapse. But please don't look so worried, Uncle Samuel. You have nothing to fear out here in the West. Neurasthenia occurs mainly in cities. Some people think it is caused by corsets, bad diets, and airlessness."

"I see," Pa said, his eyes narrowing. "I'll tell you what I think of such—"

"Well, now we know," Mother interrupted. She gave Pa a warning look. "Thank you for telling us, Elizabeth." Slowly, she lowered the unwanted bowls of peaches to the table.

"Say, I'll take those if the cousins can't eat them. I'm not afraid of no newtheenia," George said. He speared his share. His brothers and Nellie flashed their forks, too. The peaches vanished.

Mother and Pa seemed too distracted to scold the boys for impolitely reaching across the table. Addie cut her peach into small bits and ate slowly, watching Elizabeth drum her fingers on the table. Why didn't the canned fruit taste as sweet as she had imagined it would?

Pa dabbed his moustache with his napkin and pushed back his chair. "Very delicious, Becca!" he said. He scanned the remains of dinner and then looked at Elizabeth and Maudie. "Waste not, want not, that's the rule here. You girls should know that in this household we finish what's on our plates."

Addie felt so embarrassed by Pa's speech, she avoided looking at her cousins. Pa stood up and took his hat from the peg by the door. "It's time for chores. Come on, boys. There's milking to be done."

George, Lew, and Burt scooted from the table and followed Pa outdoors.

"Well now," Mother said, turning to the girls, "we'll have plenty of hands to finish the dishes, won't we?"

Elizabeth yawned and carelessly crumpled her napkin. "We never do dishes at home, do we Maudie? We have hired help for that sort of thing."

Addie squirmed and studied the table. Elizabeth had broken another household rule. No one could refuse to help with a chore.

"Well, Elizabeth," Mother said kindly, "now's as good a time as any to learn, wouldn't you say?" She secretly winked at Addie and handed her the buckets to get water from the pump. "And while we wash, we can chat about Sabula and the family."

Elizabeth and Maudie remained silent.

At the pump, Addie filled two buckets. Incredible! What would it be like to never have to wash dishes? She wished her family could afford hired help.

When she returned, Addie poured water into the kettle and set it on the stove to boil. "You can dry, all right?" she said, handing each cousin a flour-sack towel. "It's

48

really quite complicated. You rub the plate like this."

Elizabeth rolled her eyes. She did not seem to think that Addie's light-hearted demonstration was funny. But Maudie took the towel willingly.

"Now tell us all about Sabula," Mother said. She scraped the leftover bits of food from the plates into a bucket for the pigs. She poured hot water from the teakettle into two dishpans. Efficiently, she gathered all the plates and utensils and dumped them into one. With a hard chunk of yellow homemade soap, she rubbed a rag to make suds. As she washed, she handed clean dishes to Addie to rinse in the second pan. "What's new in town these days?"

"Well, let's see," Elizabeth said. "What's new? The circus came to Sabula in May. Last winter Charles Munroe, the champion skater, appeared at the Metropolitan Roller Skating Rink. Mother wouldn't allow me to go. She said I might become overexcited. The Van Buren Hotel burned down a couple weeks ago. And do you remember Martha McGann? She drowned out near Green Island. I watched them fish out her body. Of course, I never told Mother."

"How unfortunate! I'm afraid I don't remember Martha," Mother said hurriedly. "But how is your mother? It's been so long since I last saw her."

"Oh, as beautiful as ever." Elizabeth rubbed the back of a plate very hard. "Of course, she's so busy paying social calls and traveling about, we scarcely see her. Isn't that right, Maudie?"

Maudie nodded as she wiped the inside of a cup.

"And Papa, dear Papa," Elizabeth continued, "is very active with his law practice. He's often far away trying one case or another. But he never forgets to bring us expensive souvenirs. He loves us very much." Elizabeth smiled at Maudie. Maudie lost her grip, and the cup went flying.

"No harm done, Maudie," Mother said.

Maudie picked up the cup and resumed drying. But her expression remained flustered.

"Elizabeth, do you know a girl my age named Eleanor O'Neill?" Addie asked shyly. "We used to be neighbors and best friends, but she hasn't written to me in a year or so. I thought perhaps you might have met her."

"She must go to the school on the south side of town," Elizabeth replied. "We north-siders don't have anything to do with the children over there."

"Oh," said Addie. She felt disappointed and strangely homesick. She had not thought about her old friend in a long time, and now she suddenly missed her again. Good old Eleanor, always ready with some reckless scheme, some new practical joke. Why had she stopped writing? Maybe Addie had been gone so long that Eleanor just forgot about her.

"I have lots and lots of friends," Elizabeth continued. "In two years, we are all going to Sabula High School together."

"Addie's going to high school next year," Mother said, her face beaming with pride. "All the way over in Yankton."

Addie cringed.

"Will you get to wear a uniform?" Elizabeth asked. "Have you memorized your high school song yet?"

"A uniform?" Addie said. "A song?"

"For exercise class, the girls at Sabula High School wear skirts and shirtwaist blouses over full bloomers. And of course fancy sashes. Would you like to hear the Sabula High School song?" Without waiting for an answer, Elizabeth began singing in a loud, piercing voice.

On the banks of the old Mississippi River
Where the dear little flowers grow,
On the dear old bluffs we will roam forever
And look on the world down below.
We work and play the live long day
As you will surely see;
we'll show to you the way we do
In dear old Sabula, Ioway.

Elizabeth nudged her sister. "Come on, Maudie. Help me sing the chorus."

Maudie cleared her throat and sang softly.

O Sabula, dear Sabula, O, Sabula, Sabula dear,
We will always dearly love you
O Sabula, Sabula dear.

Mother applauded. "That was wonderful!"

Addie bit her lip. Miss Brophy had not mentioned anything about a Yankton High School uniform. What happened if a student wore the wrong clothes to exercise class? And what happened if someone did not know the school song on the first day?

"Elizabeth, you seem like you're already an expert on high school," Mother said. "Perhaps you and Maudie can give Addie some advice."

"Maudie doesn't go to high school anymore," Elizabeth said.

"I...I only went for a year," Maudie stammered. "Mother said I have no head for studies."

"Addie, I'd love to help you get ready for high school. It will be great fun," Elizabeth said. "I bet some of my outfits would fit you perfectly. You can try on your favorite. Then just give me a brush and some combs, and I can fix you up with my curling iron. I know all the latest hairstyles. Don't you think Addie would look better in a Saratoga Wave, Maudie? Maybe I'll give myself one, too. Then we can be twins."

Addie glowed with pleasure. Twins! Was there ever a cousin as clever as Elizabeth?

"You're very kind, Elizabeth," Mother said. "Tell us some more about news from home. I'm sure Addie would love to hear all about Grandpa Burton."

Elizabeth took a deep breath. "You mean Boppo? You know, I've called him that silly name ever since I can remember. On Sundays, I go to his house for dinner. He lets me climb up in the apple tree whenever I want, and we walk down by the river and feed the ducks. Did you do that when you lived in Sabula?"

Addie shook her head. She always called her grandfather "Grandpa Burton"—never "Boppo." Elizabeth was so lucky. The closeness she shared with their grandfather was something Addie would never have. All she could do was write letters and wait for him to write back. When would she ever be able to even see or talk with him again?

"And did Mother tell you about our new house, Aunty Becca?" Elizabeth asked.

"She mentioned it in one of her letters, I believe," Mother replied. "But it's hard to imagine anything grander than the house you lived in three years ago. That was a lovely place."

"Oh, this house is much, much better. Isn't it, Maudie?"

Maudie did not reply. Her face was bright red. Addie wondered if she was feeling homesick.

"Father just had it finished last year," Elizabeth said quickly. "It's a two-story frame house with lace curtains on the front windows and a white ceramic doorknob. It has a shingle roof and a porch that goes all the way around the front.

"Father also had a special parlor built with red floral carpets that came all the way from Brussels. There's a soft green velvet settee and a pump organ that was shipped from Chicago. The organ has a little built-in shelf at each side where we keep real glass vases with windmills painted on them. The parlor is the prettiest place in the house. But Mother always locks the door so we scarcely ever have a chance to go in there."

Addie glanced around the soddy. The main part of the house was fourteen feet wide by eighteen feet long, with one window and one door. Last year, Pa had added a pine-board lean-to, where the boys slept. The floor, which had originally been hard-packed earth sprinkled with straw, was now planks of rough lumber. There was no real privacy, except when a piece of canvas, hanging from the ceiling by a string, was drawn across the soddy to separate Pa and Mother's bed from the small cot that Addie and Nellie shared.

Because the walls were made of three-foot thick sod

bricks, the house was snug in winter and cool in summer. Except when it rained and the roof leaked muddy water, it was a cozy, secure place. Addie had always been rather proud of her family's little house. Until now.

For the first time, she was painfully aware that there were no lace curtains on the window. There was no front porch, no parlor, no pump organ. There was not even a real doorknob, just an iron latch with a leather string hanging out. In comparison with Elizabeth's house in Sabula, the soddy seemed incredibly poor and primitive.

"Addie?" Mother said, startling her, "can you help Elizabeth unpack? Maudie is going to help me in the henhouse. I want to show her how we divide the new chicks between the nests. Nellie's coming with us."

Addie and Elizabeth inched the trunk into the lean-to, where two corncob mattresses were made up with the best linens the family owned. The lean-to was to be the cousins' bedroom while they stayed at Oak Hollow.

Elizabeth opened the trunk. Carelessly, she flung treasure after treasure onto the mattresses. Stacks of dainty handkerchiefs with "E" embroidered in the corners, seven pairs of shoes, five hats, numerous hair combs and stockings, and nearly a dozen dresses of every color. The sight took Addie's breath away. Only in the Montgomery Ward Catalog had she seen so many marvelous things. Her cousin owned as many clothes as Addie, her parents, brothers, and sister put together!

"This all belongs to you?" she asked.

Elizabeth laughed. "Of course. The other trunk is filled with Maudie's things. This is nothing, really. I have three times as much at home. Mother refused to let me pack everything. Here are the books I brought for you. I hope you like them."

Addie reverently took the leather-bound copies of *Robinson Crusoe* and *Gulliver's Travels*. She flipped through the pages. "Oh, thank you! Thank you, very much. These books smell just like fresh cucumbers. They must be brand-new."

Elizabeth laughed. "Of course, silly. Do you think I'd give you used books?"

Addie could not believe it. Her very own brand-new books!

"My mother told me that you're becoming something of a writer."

Addie blushed. "Well, I have tried to write poems—"

"It must be hard to find anything poetic to write about out here, so far from civilization."

Addie felt as if she were shrinking. Miss Brophy had liked her work. But she doubted that her sophisticated cousin would be impressed with simple verses about the prairie. All thoughts of sharing her poetry with Elizabeth disappeared.

"That's strange!" Elizabeth exclaimed, peering into the trunk. Then she laughed gaily, as if something were a great joke. "Will you look at these?" She held up four silver candlesticks. "Mother's maid is becoming quite daft." She pawed down through more layers of clothes. "And here's all our monogrammed flatware! No wonder this trunk was so heavy! Mother must be frantic. She probably thinks they've been stolen."

Addie peered into the trunk. "And what about *that*?" she gasped.

Elizabeth pulled out a beautiful bisque-headed doll with blonde curls and fragile, white ceramic features. The doll was wearing a blue coat and a straw hat. She had dainty bisque hands with fingers. And on her feet she wore tiny leather boots, just like a real person.

Addie stared. "Does she belong to you?"

"Of course. This is Jessica. I have five others at home. Each one has different colored hair. But Jessica is my favorite. Do you want to hold her?"

Addie lowered the books into her lap. Speechlessly, she held out her hands. Addie's only doll, Ruby Lillian, had a china head, a painted smile, and a body made of stuffed cotton. She did not have real curls or hands with fingers. She did not even have feet. Ruby Lillian's dresses were all handmade. And she was so small, she could fit inside Addie's apron pocket. Since Addie had turned twelve, she did not play with Ruby Lillian as often. The beloved doll spent most of her time sleeping inside Addie's secret cigar box.

Such a magnificent doll as Jessica could not sleep inside a cigar box. "Does Jessica have her own real doll bed?" Addie asked.

"Certainly!" Elizabeth exclaimed. "It's made of brass and has a white canopy. But Mother said it was too large for me to bring along."

"And what about...what about her clothes?"

"She has a whole wardrobe, all store-bought dresses and hats and shoes. She even has her own little hairbrush. Of course, I had to leave all that behind, too."

Addie sighed and sat the doll in her lap. "Your doll— she winks!"

Elizabeth chuckled. "That's the way she was made. She came all the way from Paris."

"Paris, France?"

Elizabeth nodded.

A winking doll with real curls that came all the way from France! Addie wondered how she would ever be able to share Ruby Lillian with her cousin. Ruby Lillian was so simple, so unexciting.

"I have all kinds of things in Sabula. A wooden dollhouse with a hidden stairway and an attic and a little carved family. I've got a real toy stove, a washer, a toy carpet sweeper, and a miniature sewing machine that really works. I have my own croquet set and my own pair of roller skates. But I wasn't allowed to bring all those along on the train." Elizabeth paused. "You like Jessica, don't you?"

Addie nodded.

Elizabeth took Jessica back. "Well, perhaps some time I'll let you play with her." She whispered something to the doll and lifted her high. Jessica winked.

5   SILENT CRYING

When it was time for bed, Elizabeth insisted on fastening a sheet over the lean-to doorway, even though no one else was in the soddy. Addie wondered if this modest routine had something to do with—what was that disease? Newtheenia? But she was too embarrassed to ask.

"I want everyone to leave while Maudie and I get dressed in our nightgowns," Elizabeth explained.

Addie shuffled out the door with Nellie May. What else could she do?

"Pick me up!" sleepy Nellie whined.

Addie lifted her sister so that she could rest her head on her shoulder. She waved away mosquitoes. From the barn she could hear her brothers' shouts and laughter. She frowned. It did not seem fair that they were having fun while she was standing here in the dark feeling left out.

This was supposed to be a special time. She had

imagined sharing happy confidences with her cousins before bed. They might read aloud from *Gulliver's Travels* or *Robinson Crusoe,* or they could comb Jessica's beautiful hair. But nothing seemed to be working out the way she had hoped. First the pig disaster, then the dinner disappointment, and now this. Would she and Nellie May have to wait outside every night before they could get into bed?

The presence of the cousins had upset the familiar nighttime routine. Since her brothers were exiled to the barn loft, she could not whisper silly bedtime stories to them. Should she ask Mother to kiss her goodnight? Or would Elizabeth think that was babyish?

"Something's biting me," Nellie complained.

Addie paced back and forth, waving one hand at the mosquitoes. At the corner of the soddy, she stopped. She heard the low, worried murmur of her parents' voices.

"I wouldn't worry about that outlaw, Becca," Pa said quietly.

Addie strained to hear more. Were her parents as concerned as she was about the runaway?

"I'm sure he's cleared out of the county by now," Pa continued. "We've got bigger problems right here. Unless it rains soon, the hay we start cutting tomorrow is all we're going to get this year."

"You don't think we'll cut a second crop?"

"Not if this drought keeps up. We'll have to buy hay or sell cattle before next winter."

"What about the corn? What about the flax? You said they looked good."

"They did. But now I doubt the flax will bloom. And the corn is withering."

"What if we water the crops ourselves? We've got the well."

"It would be impossible. We could never carry water for twenty-five acres of corn and thirty acres of flax. And who knows how long the well will hold out?"

"We've got the creek."

"With enough heat for enough days, that could run dry, too."

"It'll rain, Samuel." Mother's whisper was insistent. "I'm *sure* it will."

"Mama?" Nellie cried. She unstuck her sweaty forehead from Addie's neck.

"Is that you, Nellie? Is Addie with you?" Mother called.

Addie stepped out of the shadows. "We're both right here."

"You girls should be in bed by now," Mother replied.

"We're waiting for Elizabeth and Maudie to get ready," Addie said.

"Well, go on inside anyway." Addie could not see Pa's face, but his voice sounded weary. "We've got a busy day ahead of us."

"Pa?"

"Yes, Addie."

Addie took a deep breath. "Did you hear anything in Defiance today about that dangerous fellow George said escaped from the train—"

"I wouldn't pay any mind to George's foolish stories, Addie," Pa interrupted. "You know how he sometimes likes to stretch the truth."

"But do you think they've caught the fellow by now?"

"There's nothing to worry about. Now get on to bed. That's an order."

"Yes, sir," Addie mumbled. "Goodnight, Pa. Goodnight, Mother." Somehow Pa's words had not convinced her.

"I'll tuck you in as soon as we check on the boys," Mother promised.

Addie carried Nellie to the soddy door and knocked.

"Addie and Nellie? You may come in now!" Elizabeth called. Addie pushed open the door, and Elizabeth poked her head out from behind the lean-to sheet. "Isn't there some way to close the curtain on that window?"

Addie lowered her sister onto the cot. She glanced at the open window. Whenever the wind blew, the gingham curtain fluttered. "I thought you didn't like airlessness. If we close the window, it will be awfully stuffy."

"I'm not worried about the air. It's that curtain I don't

like. It doesn't cover the window."

Addie scowled. After all, the gingham curtain was her own creation. She helped Nellie out of her dress into her sleeveless nightshirt. "Nobody's going to spy on you. I bet George and Lew and Burt are already snoring out there in the loft. Pa and Mother are checking them now."

"I'm not worried about your brothers. I'm worried about the sky. Can't you see how huge and black it is?"

Addie scratched her head. Elizabeth made no sense at all. Of course the prairie sky was huge and black. It was nighttime, wasn't it?

Elizabeth scurried to the window. She was dressed in a frilly white nightgown and matching lace cap that tied underneath her chin. She yanked the curtain against the window and pinned the edges to the wall with two big pearl hat pins. Maudie, wearing the same kind of cap, peeked curiously around the sheet hanging in the lean-to doorway. She made no move to help her sister.

"Look," Elizabeth said, "isn't that better?"

Maudie shrugged.

"There's nothing to be afraid of," Addie insisted. "Miry's locked up inside his pen. I don't know what you heard back in Iowa, but all the Indians I've met around here have been friendly. So you don't need to be—"

"I'm not afraid of pigs," Elizabeth snapped. "I'm not afraid of Indians. I'm not afraid of anything."

Maudie retreated into the lean-to. Elizabeth stomped in behind her, whipping the sheet closed. "I'm taking this mattress, Maudie. You can sleep on that one."

"Goodnight, Addie," Maudie called.

"Goodnight, Maudie. Goodnight, Elizabeth," Addie replied.

The corncob mattresses in the lean-to rustled and squeaked. Then there was silence.

Addie did not know what to think. In spite of all her family's special preparations, nothing seemed to have impressed her cousin. What if Elizabeth decided she hated it here? What if she wrote to Aunt Rachel and asked to come home early? That would be terrible. There was so much Elizabeth seemed to know—so much Addie could learn from her. Addie might never have another chance to become friends with someone as worldly and attractive as her cousin.

When Mother returned from the barn, she gave Nellie and Addie a goodnight kiss. She said goodnight to Maudie and Elizabeth. Then she blew out the candle that was burning on the table.

"It's too dark," Elizabeth said suddenly.

"We can't leave a candle burning all night, Elizabeth," Mother explained. "It's dangerous."

"I'm always allowed to keep a light burning in my bedroom back in Sabula."

"This isn't Sabula," Mother replied. "Now go to sleep and have pleasant dreams."

"Goodnight, Aunty Becca," Maudie replied.

Addie turned over and closed her eyes. She heard her father come inside and the canvas curtain slide shut. In a moment, she was asleep.

It must have been very late when she awoke. She heard a noise, a calling. Could it be the outlaw? She imagined him standing alone in the open prairie, raging against the world. What if he decided to use Oak Hollow as his hideout? She had to warn her brothers in the barn. She had to wake Pa and tell him to take the gun and—

"YIP - YIP - YIP - YIYEEEEEEE!"

Coyotes.

Addie sighed with relief. Two, maybe three miles away, some coyotes were howling together the way they often did on clear, warm nights. Song dogs, that was what Pa called them. The high-pitched coyote music was as mournful and wild as the wind on the open plains.

When she first had come to Dakota, the sound had frightened Addie. But now that she had finally grown used to the coyotes' song, it seemed as familiar as the chitter and buzz of crickets. Sometimes she listened for the coyotes the way she remembered listening for the midnight whistle of the last train through Sabula.

For a moment, her eyelids shut. Then, from the lean-to, she heard another noise. Someone was crying.

"Maudie, is that you?" Addie whispered. Her older cousin seemed so timid and woeful.

The whimpering stopped.

Addie waited and listened in the stuffy darkness. Then, she bravely whispered, "Elizabeth?"

No one answered.

Finally, unable to keep her eyes open any longer, Addie nudged Nellie and turned wearily on her side. But before she drifted off to sleep, she prayed for her cousin's quick recovery from homesickness. "Whichever cousin—Maudie or Elizabeth," she said, then added, "and please send the outlaw far away from here. And please, God, please, let it rain."

6 BARN CONCERT

"George! Lew! Burt!" Pa shouted. "Addie! Come on and get up now!"

Addie opened her eyes, rolled out of bed, and got dressed. Although Pa didn't shout the cousins' names, she could hear them getting up, too. How could anyone stay asleep through Pa's bellowing wake-up call?

Addie knew Pa had been up for a long time. He already would have oiled and greased the mower and sharpened the five-foot sickle. Once the dew dried, he would head out with the clattering, horse-drawn mower and begin cutting the ten acres of wild clover, big bluestem, Indian grass, and switch grass that grew out on the bog to the south. Every day for the next two weeks, from dawn till dusk, the family and a hired man would labor in the heat and dust to turn the field into enormous haystacks—cattle feed for the coming winter.

There was no coolness in the morning air. Dust hovered

like a grey smear over the horizon, and the wind carried the smell of a distant prairie fire. The day promised the kind of blistering weather that made haying nearly unbearable. Before breakfast, it was the boys' turn to bring in the eight milk cows from the pasture near the creek, where the livestock stayed at night. George, Lew, and Burt whistled and hollered and waved sticks. Maybe the delicious smell of frying sidemeat filled them with energy. Or maybe it was something else.

"You're sure showing off for Elizabeth and Maudie, aren't you, George?" Addie called from the pump. The boys forced the cows along at such a pace that milk spurted from their full, swinging udders. "Better slow down before Pa sees you running the herd like that."

George acted as if he hadn't heard Addie. He didn't look up as he passed the cousins, who huddled half-awake near the house. They wore matching pink satin dresses. Mother had warned Elizabeth and Maudie that their fancy outfits would be ruined during morning chores. "These are our everyday dresses back home," Elizabeth replied. Her peevish tone of voice made it clear that she never expected to be milking on her first day in Dakota.

"Come on, Ugly Cow! Get! Get!" George waved his stick at the milker with the strange, mottled brown and black markings. Ugly Cow made a dash to snatch a few green tips of buffalo grass near Mother's shade trees. Addie motioned to her cousins to follow her as she slipped through the gate into the empty corral in front of the barn. Addie was careful to latch the corral gate behind them.

The cows knew what to do without any prompting. They thundered to the moss-lined stock tank near the pump and drank with great slurps and slobbers. Then the enormous creatures headed toward the corral. They lowed and flapped their tails, scratching themselves on the fence. Gleaming, biting flies covered their backs and clung to their ears like so many black earrings.

Addie hurried to the big barn door. When she opened it, out poured an overpowering smell of cow, hay, and manure. Elizabeth and Maudie climbed on the fence and held their noses.

"Ready?" George called.

Addie waved and swung wide the barn door. "Here they come!" she warned her cousins. George opened the gate. The bellowing cows shoved and pushed through the corral. Ugly Cow butted a young Brown Swiss out of her way and led the herd into the dark, stuffy barn. She was boss cow, and none of the others had better forget it.

"Come on!" Addie shouted to her cousins after the rest of the herd had followed Ugly Cow inside. Each cow went automatically to its own stanchions, upright wooden bars that fit comfortably on either side of the cow's neck to confine it to its stall. Lined up in a row, the cows were in easy reach of a long, wooden trough. When Burt and Lew sprinkled the trough with ground meal and fresh hay, the cows pushed against the stanchions until the wood squeaked. With their long, rough, grey tongues, they swept the trough for every crumb, every wisp. Their strong jaws ground from side to side as they chewed their breakfast.

"Here are your pails," Burt said, handing them to Addie, Maudie, and Elizabeth.

"You know what to do?" Lew asked the two cousins. Maudie shook her head and looked frankly perplexed. But Elizabeth put her hands on her hips and said, "These cows are dirty. How can you expect me to milk such filthy beasts? And what about all these flies?"

Impatiently, George waved his arm at the cloud of blood-thirsty insects. "The cows are dirty because the coolest place to be right now is standing belly-deep in the muddy part of the creek. Before you can milk, you've got to wash the udders."

"Wash the udders?" Elizabeth replied. "I'd rather die."

Addie sighed. "I'll wash the cow for you and show you what to do." She sat down on a three-legged stool beside Bess, the milker least likely to kick anybody in the teeth. With a bucket of water, she gently washed the rank-smelling mud from the cow's udder. When she finished, she noticed a lump on Bess's back. "George, can you come over here a minute?"

George took one look at the lump and shook his head. Expertly, he used two fingers and squeezed. Out popped something small and black and wriggling.

"What in heaven's name is that?" Elizabeth demanded.

"It *was* a heel-fly grub," George said, delighted by the disgust on Elizabeth's face, "but now it's dead." He tossed the creature over his shoulder and went back to milking.

Maudie gasped. Elizabeth squeezed her eyes shut tight for a moment and groaned.

"Heel-fly grubs look hideous," Addie agreed. "But if we can get rid of them, the cows feel better." She positioned the bucket under Bess's udder. "You and Maudie come over here so you can see what I'm doing."

The two cousins crouched reluctantly beside Addie. Without warning, Bess's hard, heavy tail swung around and clobbered Elizabeth. Addie tried not to laugh. "I guess somebody's going to have to hold Bess's tail to keep it out of our way."

Elizabeth wiped the front of her dress and shook her head. "Not me."

"I'll do it." Maudie cautiously picked up Bess's tail, which was clodded with lumps of dried dirt. Bess turned her head as far as she could inside the stanchions and with big brown eyes stared soulfully at Maudie. "Poor thing!" Maudie whispered.

"What do you mean, 'poor thing'?" Elizabeth demanded. "What about poor us? Addie, show us how to finish this job so we can get out of here."

"Watch closely," Addie explained. She leaned against Bess to reach the teats on the far side of the udder. The cow's big belly gave off heat like a furnace. "You use your thumb and forefinger like this." She grasped the cow's swollen teat at the top with her two fingers and then gently tugged downward, gradually closing her fist. As the teat emptied, milk squirted repeatedly into the metal pail. *Ting, ting, ting.* "See? It's not so hard. You just do the same thing for all four teats until they're empty."

Elizabeth sat down primly on the milking stool and arranged the folds of her fine skirt. Gingerly, she clutched the teat and pulled. Nothing happened.

"Watch me again. Just squeeze gently. Like this."

Elizabeth tried a second time. A tiny stream of milk dribbled into the bucket.

"That's it!" Addie said encouragingly.

Elizabeth did not seem the least pleased. She tugged and grumbled, "At this rate, I won't finish milking until midnight."

"It takes some getting used to. But before you know it, you'll be just as fast as the rest of us. Maudie, do you want to try?" Addie asked.

Elizabeth seemed more than happy to give up the

milking stool to her sister. Maudie sat down and moved her big hands the way Addie had shown her. Milk streamed into the bucket.

"Good for you!" Addie said. A grin surfaced for a split second on Maudie's face.

"How much longer?" Elizabeth complained. "Hurry up!"

Addie moved to the next stall where Jezebel waited. She was irritated by Elizabeth's ungrateful whining. Her cousin was not helping. Yet there she stood, demanding that the rest of them hurry.

Slowly, the *twing, twing, twing, twang* changed to *twash, twash, twash, twash* as the buckets filled with warm, sweet-smelling milk and frothy foam. Addie stopped milking for a moment. What was that? Accompanying the rhythmic sound of *twash, twash, twash* was a faint melody. Yes, someone was softly whistling "Yankee Doodle." Addie leaned over and peeked into Bess's stall. The music was coming from Maudie!

"...riding on a po-ny," Addie sang along. "Stuck a feather in his hat—"

"and called it macaron-i!" George joined in.

"Yankee Doodle keep it up," Burt and Lew warbled. "Yankee Doodle Dan-dy! Mind your manners and your step and with the girls be han-dy!"

After three more verses of "Yankee Doodle," two

versions of "Down by the Old Mill Stream," and a rollicking rendition of "I've Been Working on the Railroad," George broke in with his own solo.

Hurrah for Dakota, the land of the free
The home of the grasshopper, bedbug and flea.
I'll holler its praises and sing of its fame
While starving to death on a government claim.

My clothes are all ragged, my language is rough,
My bread is case-hardened, both solid and tough,
The dough is scattered all over the room,
And the floor would get scared at the sight of a broom.

How happy I am on my government claim,
I've nothing to lose, I've nothing to gain,
I've nothing to eat, and I've nothing to wear,
And nothing from nothing is honest and fair.

"George, where did you learn such a despicable song?" Addie demanded.

"From some of the fellows at school," he said, grinning from ear to ear. "I'm pretty musical, don't you think? Some day I'm going to get my own instrument. Then you'll hear some really good tunes and—"

"Since we're finished," Elizabeth interrupted, "can we

finally eat breakfast now?" Not once had she joined in the milking or the singing.

"We should give cow concerts more often!" Lew smiled at Maudie as he and Burt hoisted a full, heavy bucket. Together the boys carried the milk to the root cellar, where it would be stored while the cream separated.

George laughed. "Even Ugly Cow liked the music. Notice how she's smiling?"

Ugly Cow turned her bossy head. Her cowbell rattled.

"Cows can't smile," Elizabeth said with authority.

"How do you know, Princess Newtheenia?" George replied.

Elizabeth did not answer. She flipped her curls and stomped empty-handed out of the barn.

"You shouldn't have called her that, George," Addie said, even though she could not help smiling.

"She won't stay mad long," Maudie said quietly. She stepped out from the stall and patted Bess. "Why don't you let me carry something?"

Addie and George exchanged looks of surprise as Maudie hauled two full buckets of milk out of the barn. "Well, I'll be!" Addie whispered. "She's sure strong for a city girl."

George nodded. "How do you like that? And here I thought all she could say was yes, no, please, and thank-you!"

7 SECRET PLACE, SECRET CLUB

Just as Maudie had predicted, Elizabeth seemed herself again by the time Mother served breakfast. "I don't think there's much danger from neurasthenia out here in the country," Elizabeth said as she sat down at the table. "I'm sure Mother would say it was all right for us to eat this."

The cousins each finished two helpings of flapjacks with sorghum syrup. Addie felt relieved that Elizabeth's appetite and good humor had returned.

"Somebody's coming!" Burt hollered. He stood in the doorway wiping crumbs and syrup from his face. The other children ran outside. Coming toward them was the silhouette of a large man partially obscured by a rolling cloud of dust.

Addie sharply drew in her breath. She peered hard for some dreaded sign—perhaps a six-shooter slung low on the hip. But the longer she watched, the more certain she became that this early morning visitor was not the runaway outlaw. It was only Tilla's brother Ole, coming to help Pa with the haying.

"Hello, Ole!" George called, and waved.

Ole, who stood more than six feet tall, was a shy, homely giant. As usual, he refused to come into the house. He stood in the yard, shuffling his big feet. As he muttered something Addie could not understand, the gap between his front teeth showed.

Pa hired Ole regularly to help with haying and threshing. "You're a hard worker and as strong as three men," Pa liked to tell him. "You ought to find yourself a good wife and settle down." The first time Tilla had translated Pa's words into Norwegian for her brother, how Ole had blushed!

Today Ole's job was to circle the field and cut hay with the extra mower Pa had borrowed from Mr. Fency. Then Ole and Pa would rake, pitch, and stack with help from the rest of the family.

Last year, when there had been plenty of rain, Addie had thought haying seemed never-ending. Soon after the June hay was harvested, the grass grew back and the whole grueling process had to be repeated in late August. But this year, instead of coming up to her waist, the grass on the bog barely reached her knees. Unless it rained soon, they'd only cut one crop. And the grass was so dry that lightning could start the whole field on fire.

Mother stepped outside the soddy. "Good morning, Ole."

Ole removed his battered blue cap, revealing a thatch of white-blond hair. *"Goddag,"* he mumbled. His pale blue eyes darted toward the doorway.

"Samuel's out in the field." Mother pointed to the distant mower.

"Ya, ya." Ole bobbed his head as if he understood.

"Can you take him a few more burlap sacks and another jug of water?" Mother asked. "I'm afraid that's all we have in case of fire—"

Ole's face turned bright red. What had Mother said to make him blush that way? Addie turned just in time to see Maudie, silent as a water bug, scuttle through the doorway into the soddy.

"Well, well," Mother murmured.

Elizabeth came outside to meet Ole. "Please excuse my sister's manners," she said brightly. "My name's Elizabeth Nichols. How do you do?" She held out her hand.

Ole stared at Elizabeth's outstretched hand as if she were offering him a live rattlesnake. Without another word, he jammed on his hat and hurried toward the field.

"What an unfriendly foreign fellow!" Elizabeth said. "Maudie, you can come out now. He's gone."

Addie watched Mother smile and shake her head. What was so funny? Since Mother seemed to be in such a good mood, maybe now was the moment to ask a favor. "Mother? Until Pa and Ole cut enough hay so that we can begin stacking, do you think I could show Elizabeth around the farm—maybe take her down to Rattling Creek?"

"As long as you finish your chores," Mother replied. "Would you like to go, Elizabeth?"

Elizabeth shrugged. "I suppose so."

"What about you, Maudie?" Mother called. "Would you like to go to the creek with Addie?"

Addie hoped Maudie would refuse. She wanted this to be a special trip, just her and Elizabeth.

Maudie peeked through the doorway. She shook her head shyly.

"Then you and I can stay right here and start supper," Mother said. "I'm going to show you how to make bread. We'll have a lovely chat while Addie and Elizabeth are gone. Addie, be back in an hour or so, will you?"

Addie nodded. Now she could show Elizabeth the secret place! She knew she was betraying Tilla by revealing their favorite spot beside the creek. But somehow that did not matter. She just had to impress her grown-up, capable cousin who seemed to know so many important things.

The trail through the pasture rippled with heat. The sun bore down through Addie's cotton sunbonnet, inside her scalp, right into her very brain. Dust puffed up at each footstep.

"Is Dakota always this hot?" Elizabeth asked, rubbing her eyes. "And this wind! Back home I can put on my little peaked felt hat and it will stay just right all day. But I could never wear such a darling hat here!"

"It's not always so hot. Sometimes it gets pretty cold and snowy. See the piece of turkey-red calico tied high in that cottonwood branch?"

"You mean that little rag fluttering way up there?"

Addie nodded. "Two years ago the winter was so snowy that George climbed a drift to reach that spot."

"I don't believe you."

"It's true. You can ask him."

Elizabeth took one last look and followed Addie through the peach willows and underbrush. Along the sheltered creek bottom, morning light filtered through the leaves of cottonwoods, shrub willows, wild plum, and wild cherry trees, creating dappled, sleepy shadows. To give Elizabeth a complete tour of Rattling Creek, Addie took the long way to her secret place.

The girls walked downstream. They stopped to peer inside the caved-in places in the low cutbank where crayfish scuttled and hid. A swallow-tailed kite dove for a frog, but the frog plopped into the water just in time.

"Come on!" Addie whispered, glad at last to see a

smile on Elizabeth's face. "Cooler here, isn't it?"

Elizabeth nodded. She pointed to a large slime-covered mud hole in the pasture a few yards from the water. "What's that?" With the tip of her boot, she poked the surface. "Kind of trembles like tomato aspic, doesn't it? But it smells much worse."

"It's a sinkhole. Better step back—you don't want to get too close."

Elizabeth picked up a rock and hurled it into the middle of the sinkhole. The ground gasped and slowly swallowed the rock with a soft glub. "Why can't I get too close?"

"Because it's dangerous. One of our calves walked in and never came out. All Pa found were the hoof marks. And when he stuck a twenty-foot pole in there, he couldn't reach bottom."

Elizabeth's eyes grew wide. She tossed another rock. "I wonder where it goes. I wonder how many bones are down there."

Addie shivered. She did not like the sinkhole. It was a mysterious, evil place to be avoided. "Come on. Let's cross on these stones and follow the bank upstream. I want to show you something nice—my very own secret spot."

When they finally reached the bend in the creek, Elizabeth sat down on the grass. "So this is it? Very nice." She pulled off her fancy boots and wiggled her toes in the stream. "I can see why you always go barefoot. It's much more comfortable. Have you noticed that I never sweat? I trained myself not to."

"You did?" Addie asked. "How?"

Elizabeth gathered up her dress and tied it around her waist. She tore off the borrowed apron Mother had given her and twisted it around her head like a turban. "You must con-cen-trate," she said in an eerie voice. *"Con-cen-trate."*

Addie giggled.

Elizabeth waded into the water up to her knees. "Remember that old nursery rhyme?

Mother, may I go out to swim?
Yes, my darling daughter.
Hang your clothes on a hickory limb
And don't go near the water.

Addie moved her feet back and forth in the cool current. "I know that rhyme."

"Well, I'm going out to swim, and I'm not hanging my clothes on any hickory limb." Elizabeth waded out past her knees to her waist. "I always used to go swimming in the river, but I never told my mother. She would have been terribly hysterical. She says young ladies should only swim in 'respectable water places.' But I used to swim in the Mississippi, even though the current is much stronger and more dangerous than this. I was never afraid." She held her nose, sat down, and disappeared. Her turban floated away, and her dark hair drifted like willow leaves. Her pink satin dress puffed and billowed.

"Elizabeth?" Addie called. "That's enough. Come up now."

Five seconds, ten seconds, twenty seconds passed, and still there was no sign of Elizabeth.

"Come out this instant!" Addie shouted. One bubble, then two, three popped on the surface. "Elizabeth!" she screamed, and plunged into the creek. She grabbed her cousin and tried to drag her to shore. Why did Elizabeth seem so heavy? Was she *dead?* "Elizabeth! *Elizabeth!*"

Elizabeth exploded up out of the water. She spouted a mouthful of water and laughed and laughed.

"Why did you do that?" Addie demanded.

"Do what?" her cousin asked innocently. Her hair hung in limp strands, and her beautiful dress was muddy and ruined.

"Try to trick me into thinking you were drowning. That wasn't very funny. And look at *me!* Now I'm all wet, too!"

"You most certainly are! You look like a wet rat. Say, I just had a spectacular idea. Since this is our own secret place, let's start our own secret club. Just the two of us,

85

nobody else. I'll be president. You can be secretary."

A secret club! Addie wrung out the skirt of her dress and smiled. She could easily forgive Elizabeth's prank for a chance to be in her secret club. Just the two of them. She'd rather be president and let Elizabeth be secretary, but perhaps after a while they could trade. The main thing was to make sure Tilla never found out. Tilla wouldn't understand. She'd get angry and ruin everything.

"What should we call our club?" Elizabeth said. "We must think of a clever name. How about the 'Wet Rats'?"

Addie giggled. She cupped her hands and gave her cousin a tremendous splash. Elizabeth shrieked and splashed her back. "Now do you want to see another secret?" Addie asked, suddenly feeling very bold. "It's something really special."

"As the president of the Wet Rat Club, I command you to show me!"

"Wait here. I'll be back as fast as I can!"

Even without stopping, it took Addie nearly fifteen minutes to run all the way to the barn. She slipped inside and grabbed the cigar box from its hiding place, then raced back to the creek. "Look!" she gasped, out of breath. She plopped down beside Elizabeth and opened the box.

First, out came Ruby Lillian. How comforting her doll's dear old face seemed! All-knowing, all-forgiving, she smiled up at Addie. There was a hint of mischief in her blue eyes.

"Who's that?" Elizabeth asked.

"Ruby Lillian. How do you like her?"

"Very sweet. Rather rustic. If we fix her up, she might make a nice little *cameriste* for my Jessica."

*"Cama-*what?"

Elizabeth laughed. "Come, come, Addie. Surely you must know a little French if you're going to high school. *La cameriste* is a proper lady's maid."

"Oh," Addie said, embarrassed she knew no French. And how humiliating to think of Ruby Lillian as Jessica's servant! Addie tucked her doll back inside the box.

"What else do you have in there?"

Addie cleared her throat. "This might not look very impressive, but it's special to me," she said shyly. She pulled out a necklace made of beads and a feather. "This was given to me by Indians when we first came here three years ago. I was all alone taking care of my two brothers."

Elizabeth eagerly fingered the beads. "Weren't you terrified they'd scalp you?"

"The Indians were hungry. All I did was give them some cornbread and beans. They left this in payment. I wasn't scared a bit," she boasted.

"What kind of feather is this?"

"An eagle feather. Pa told me that's the kind only the most courageous braves are allowed to wear. I think it might be magic, don't you?"

Elizabeth nodded. Not once did her eyes leave the necklace.

"Would you like to try it on?" Addie lifted the necklace over her cousin's head.

Elizabeth beamed. "How do I look?"

"Like a very brave Wet Rat."

"May I keep it?"

Addie blinked hard. She had only meant to show her cousin the necklace, not to give it to her. Surely Elizabeth wasn't serious.

"Remember, I'm your guest," Elizabeth persisted. "If I let you play with Jessica, the least you can do is give me this old necklace. All right?"

Addie didn't answer. She pretended to be preoccupied wringing out her dress. Couldn't Elizabeth tell she was upset? But how could she say no to her? If she stayed silent long enough, perhaps her cousin would realize that she did not want to give away the necklace.

"Then it's settled," Elizabeth said, smiling with satisfaction. "The necklace is mine."

"But I didn't—"

"Say, what's that?" Elizabeth poked her finger inside the open cigar box, past the stack of folded pages containing Addie's poetry, right to the envelope addressed "Board of Examiners, Yankton High School."

8 TILLA

Addie slammed the cigar box shut. How could she have been so careless?

"You're hiding something, aren't you?" Elizabeth said softly.

"No, I'm not. It's just that I don't think you'd find an old letter from...from my friend Eleanor very interesting."

Elizabeth's eyes narrowed. "I'm sure I'd find your old letter quite fascinating. We can make a trade. That old letter for this necklace. What do you say?" She fingered the eagle feather.

Addie was stunned. But she knew she had no choice. She'd have to let cunning Elizabeth keep the necklace or allow her to see what was really inside that envelope. "You can wear it, Elizabeth," she said grudgingly. "I don't—"

"Addie! Elizabeth!" Lew and Burt shouted. They staggered wild-eyed out from the underbrush.

Addie had never felt so pleased to be interrupted by her pesky brothers. "What's the matter?" she asked, hiding the cigar box under her apron.

"He's coming this way!" Burt blurted.

Lew nodded eagerly. "We've got to hide! Hurry!"

Elizabeth jumped up. "What's all this fuss about? Who's coming?"

"The runaway outlaw!" Burt hollered. Without another word, he and Lew dashed to the nearest cottonwood and began climbing.

"The runaway what?"

The outlaw! Addie didn't stop to think. "There isn't time to explain. We've got to find a place he won't get us!"

"Where?"

"Follow me!" With her box under her arm, Addie ran upstream. Quickly, she found the cottonwood that she and Tilla had nailed with board slats. The slats made a ladder up the tree trunk. "Come on, Elizabeth!"

Swiftly, the two girls scrambled up to the highest, broadest branch. They peeked through the leaves.

The only movement below was the rushing of water. Minutes seemed to drag. "I don't see anyone," Elizabeth whispered nervously. "If he finds us, will he shoot us?"

"Be quiet!" Addie warned. "I hear someone coming."

Rattle! Crunch! Crash! Leaves trembled. Branches broke.

Then, through the peach willows across the creek, she caught sight of a dark felt hat. A long stick shot out and thrashed violently. "Where are they? I just saw them. Where did they go?" a low voice growled.

Addie's heart beat wildly. Her arms seemed to be made of India rubber. Any minute she expected to lose her grip and drop out of the tree. She glanced at Elizabeth. Her cousin was biting her lower lip so hard that a trickle of blood had formed in the corner of her mouth.

"Come on out here you little rascals, you little—"

Something grunted loudly and furiously. Suddenly, the stick flew into the water, and the dark hat sailed into a chokecherry bush.

Miry burst into view. He careened through the underbrush and knocked the big-bellied figure head over heels. Arms waved. Splash! The figure fell into the water.

"Help!" he yelled, his voice now strangely high-pitched. Corncobs spilled from inside his shirt.

"George Sydney Mills!" Addie screamed. "How dare you? How dare you scare us like that?"

George sat up in the middle of the stream. He looked soggy but not at all sorry.

"You should have seen the girls' faces, George!" Lew hooted. He and Burt were laughing so hard they nearly tumbled out of their tree-top hiding place.

"'O-O-O! We've got to hide, Elizabeth!'" Burt said

in a mocking, shrill voice.

"Addie, we sure fooled you!" George grinned with great satisfaction.

Addie was so angry her face was bright red. She and Elizabeth climbed down from the tree. "There was absolutely nothing funny about what you just did, George. Nothing funny at all."

Lew and Burt howled with delight. "Don't be sore, Addie," Lew cried.

"Yea, it was just a joke," Burt added.

"Everything would have worked just perfectly if Miry hadn't followed George and bumped him into the creek," Lew said. The pig paid no attention to the children. He was too busy gobbling all the corncobs he could find.

"Come on, Elizabeth," Addie said. Furiously, she tucked the cigar box under her arm and marched back upstream toward the soddy. "Do you see what I have to put up with? You're lucky you don't have any brothers."

"You're absolutely right. Your brothers are really awful."

Addie was pleased to hear Elizabeth agree with her. For once, she and Elizabeth understood each other.

"But you have to admit it was funny when that pig pushed George into the creek," Elizabeth said, giggling. "I nearly burst right out laughing."

"You did?" Addie tried, but she could not find George's practical joke the least bit amusing. It was humiliating

92

to think that Lew and Burt had managed to trick her into believing in their "outlaw."

Suddenly, a voice called out, "Addie? Vere are you?"

"Oh, no," Addie muttered. What else could go wrong today?

"Hello," said Tilla, shyly. Balancing on one foot like an awkward, one-legged bird, she kept her eyes fixed on the bunch of dusty wild roses in her dirty hand. "I didn't know you'd have company vit you, Addie. Can I talk to you alone?"

Addie shook her head. "Anything you have to say you can say in front of my cousin, Elizabeth. Elizabeth, this is Tilla."

"Pleased to meet you, I'm sure," Elizabeth murmured in an amused voice.

Tilla coughed nervously. "Addie, I...I came to say I vas sorry for yesterday. For vat I said. Maybe I'm a little yellous."

"Yellous?" Elizabeth chuckled.

Tilla scowled at her.

"It's all right," Addie replied. If only she could hurry Tilla on her way before Elizabeth revealed that she had been to their secret place. "How are you going to walk home in only one shoe?"

Tilla broke into a grin. "You like it?" On one foot she wore a worn, orange felt slipper decorated with bright gold thread. "I find dis on de road."

Addie sighed. Tilla seemed so foolish, so unsophisticated. Surely Elizabeth would think she was ridiculous. "It looks too big for you. And what happened to the other one?"

Tilla shrugged. "One slipper better dan no slipper at all."

"Tilla, what are you doing here?" Addie asked, barely able to conceal her irritation.

"I come vit de extra harness Ole forgot. De flowers I bring for you. I know you like dese roses best." Tilla handed the flowers to Addie, then turned to Elizabeth. "So," she said, "you are de cousin who is not staying forever?"

Elizabeth smiled. "The way you talk is quite charming."

Tilla's eyes narrowed.

"Of course I am not staying forever," Elizabeth continued. "In fact, I would go home immediately if I could. But here I am, marooned in Dakota. So I must make the best of it. Stiff upper lip and all that."

"Stiff upper vat?" Tilla stared at Elizabeth's upturned mouth.

"It's just an expression. A figure of speech."

"Vat happened to your clothes? Your hair is all muddy. You don't look anyting like de fine cousin Addie tell me about."

Elizabeth chuckled. "Please excuse my soggy appearance. Addie and I have just been swimming in our very own secret place." Elizabeth's hand fluttered to the Indian necklace around her neck.

"Addie, you haf took her to de secret place?" Tilla whispered.

Addie nodded. Her ears felt hot, and she wished she could disappear. How many times had she and Tilla promised each other never, never to tell anyone the exact location of their secret place?

Tilla turned to Elizabeth. "And dat necklace. Who giff you dat?"

"Why Addie, of course."

Tilla looked at Addie in bewilderment. "You told me you never giff dat to nobody. Nobody in de vorld."

"Well, I—" Addie stammered.

"The reason Addie gave me this necklace," Elizabeth interrupted, "is because I am the president of our secret club."

"President?" Tilla asked. "Vat secret club?"

Elizabeth smiled. "Of course, it wouldn't be secret if I told you, would it? All I can reveal is that Addie is the secretary and I am the president. We are the only two members. It's a very exclusive organization."

"Exclusif?"

"Allow me to explain in plain English so that you can understand. *Exclusive* means we can belong and you can't."

Tilla shifted her weight to her other foot. "Maybe I be going," she murmured. For several moments she did not move, as if waiting for the other girls to ask her to stay.

Elizabeth tapped her toe and rolled her eyes.

"Goodbye, Tilla," Addie said, taking her cousin's cue.

Slowly, Tilla removed her lone, gaudy slipper. Then she turned and trudged barefoot across the field.

"Goodbye, Tilla," Elizabeth called cheerfully.

Tilla did not answer. As she walked farther and farther away, rising waves of heat blurred her outline until she looked more like a ghost than a real person.

Elizabeth folded her arms. "Well, I'm certainly glad you told that crude, ignorant girl to go away. Imagine her making fun of *my* appearance. Did you see that comical shoe she was wearing? Someone like her could never be in our secret club. Just look at those pathetic flowers she gave you. They're already falling apart."

Something caught in Addie's throat when she glanced down at the wild roses in her fist. In the searing sunlight, the tender petals had wilted and fallen to the ground like pink snow.

9 PRETTY AND ELEGANT

"Hold still!" Elizabeth commanded.

"I *am* holding still," said Addie. She was perched on a fallen branch in the secret place along Rattling Creek. Elizabeth stood behind her, brushing and brushing Addie's hair. Addie blinked back tears. She felt as if she were being scalped. Sweat trickled down her neck. She tried to wriggle her toes. But the dainty green boots she had borrowed from her cousin pinched dreadfully. Why did being fashionable have to be so painful?

Addie had been waiting for this moment for the past two weeks, ever since that night when Elizabeth had promised to give her a new hairstyle and allow her to try on whichever outfit she thought prettiest. Addie's favorite shoes were the pointed lace-up boots with fancy tasseled ties. The dress she had selected was a princess-style gown of pale yellow organdy with a lace ruffle around the neck and a big green bow on the bustle.

Addie's new hairstyle and outfit were to be a surprise for the rest of the family. Elizabeth had insisted on working in privacy, by the creek. Who would have thought that creating a fancy French hair style could take so long?

Addie winced with each brush stroke. Her cousin hummed. Clearly, Elizabeth enjoyed hairstyling. She certainly never acted like this when it was time to do regular chores around the farm. After two weeks, churning butter was the only job she would perform without complaining. That was because she could sit indoors to do it. "Bright sun burns my sensitive skin," Elizabeth had told the family. "Field work is out of the question. Neurasthenia may have weakened my spine. Doctors have told me to avoid sudden, strenuous movement."

Maudie paid no heed to her sister. In two weeks, her face was tinged with new color from working outdoors so much. "Maudie, farm life agrees with you," Mother said. And it was true. The mysterious crying Addie heard the first night had never returned. Maudie had become an expert milker. She seemed to enjoy caring for the chickens. And in spite of the hot weather, she regularly volunteered to stir the laundry in the kettle filled with boiling water.

"Addie!"

Addie jumped in her seat.

"Are you holding the curling iron properly?" Elizabeth

demanded. "The metal has to be hot enough or it isn't going to work."

Addie adjusted the long, thin, pencil-shaped curling iron over the flame of the candle she'd stuck in the ground.

"Your hair is very thick and coarse," Elizabeth said, "but when I'm finished, I think you'll see a lovely change. Now don't move! When I go to high school, I'm going to wear a new hairdo, too. Maybe just like this."

Addie tightly gripped the curling iron. High school. No matter what was happening, those two horrible words seemed to creep into the conversation.

Snip! Snip! Hair fell into Addie's lap, just missing the lit candle. She squirmed and looked up. "You didn't tell me you were going to cut my hair!"

Elizabeth smiled, waving Mother's shears. "I don't have much choice. If you want this hairstyle, you have to have bangs."

Addie sighed.

"See here, don't look so morose. I only cut a little in front." She stood back to admire her work. From her pocket she produced a small, blue bottle.

"What's that?" Addie asked nervously.

"An expensive setting solution I ordered from an advertisement in *Godey's Lady Book*. Hold still and shut your eyes." Elizabeth poured the solution into her cupped hand and rubbed it onto the front section of Addie's hair.

"Phew!" Addie gasped. "What is that stuff?"

"On the label it says 'carbonate of potassium, ammonia, glycerine, spirit, and rose-water.'" Elizabeth flicked a strand of wet hair straight up with the comb. "Now hand me the curling iron. And hold still."

Addie tried not to breathe as Elizabeth wound the first section of hair around the hot curling iron. After each curl was formed, the iron had to be reheated. Elizabeth worked very intently. "This hairstyle," she announced, "is starting to look just like a picture I saw in *Godey's Lady Book.*"

Addie felt encouraged. "Can I see myself?"

"Not until I'm completely finished. I left my mirror at the house anyway."

"When will you be finished? Mother said I've got to help Pa with haying this morning."

"I'm working as quickly as I can. Your back is slumped again. Do remember your posture."

Addie sucked in her stomach. She swayed her back in the fashionable way that Elizabeth had shown her.

"Your posture is much better than Maudie's. I am constantly having to remind her how to walk and sit and stand like a lady. Since she's been here, her posture is even worse. You can blow out that candle now." Elizabeth held three hair pins in the side of her mouth. She tugged, twisted, and coiled two back sections of Addie's hair, then poked her head with the hairpins.

"Ow!"

"Really, Addie. You don't need to complain quite so much. Now here's the dress. You can try it on behind that bush. Don't get it muddy."

As Addie slipped the frothy yellow dress over her head, she caught a glimpse of Elizabeth arranging the eagle feather around her neck. Addie frowned, remembering the day she had been forced to give her the necklace. That was two weeks ago—the same terrible day she had said goodbye to Tilla. She felt ashamed about what she had done. How she missed her old friend!

"What's taking you so long?" Elizabeth called.

Addie struggled with the last pearl button and stepped out from behind the bush. "How do I look?"

"Turn around so I can see your hair from all angles," Elizabeth said, squinting critically. "For a proper job, I should add some artificial flowers and strands of beads on top. But I haven't got any...now don't touch it."

"Why not?" Addie quickly withdrew her hand. Her hair felt stiff and unfamiliar.

"You might destroy my creation. Let's go. Pick the skirt up all the way in front so it doesn't drag. I'll hold the back. Aren't you excited? Wait till everyone sees you."

Filled with anticipation, Addie hurried along the path. At last, she felt pretty and elegant.

"Addie!" Mother called.

Addie quickened her pace. "Coming, Mother!"

"You look a fine sight!" Elizabeth whispered. "I'll go get the mirror."

Suddenly, George poked his mocking face out of the soddy window. "What in the world happened, Addie? You look like you've been struck by lightning."

Addie held her head high and walked confidently. What did George know? But as she took a few more steps, her ankles buckled. At the last moment, she caught her balance.

"She doesn't look like she's been struck by lightning," Burt said, pushing up beside George. "She looks like somebody plastered a jug handle on her head. See how her hair sticks out?"

Addie pretended not to hear. A sudden gust of wind jiggled her hair and buffeted the big green bow on her dress.

"What you got stuffed in the back of that dress?" George asked. "A litter of dead cats?"

"For your information," she said coolly, "this is a bustle. It's the very latest fashion."

George hooted. "You're going to look pretty silly in that get-up riding a mower."

"Shut up," Addie snapped. "I'm not wearing these clothes haying. Elizabeth is just letting me try them on."

"Well, Addie, what do we have here?" Mother said from the doorway.

Elizabeth returned with the mirror. She gave Addie a little nudge. "Posture, posture," she prompted.

Addie pushed out her chest and swayed her back.

"My, my, my!" Mother put her hand to her mouth to stifle a grin.

Addie panicked. Why was mother smiling like that?

"Here's the mirror," said Elizabeth.

Addie grabbed the mirror. "Oh, no!" she gasped. A frizzed fringe of hair hung comically over her forehead. Snakelike coils looped across the top of her head. When she turned, she caught sight of her reflection in the window glass. There she stood, swallowed up by the too-big yellow dress. The tall ruffle collar came nearly to her ears. The sleeves drooped around her knuckles. What had Elizabeth done to her? She did not look like a grown-up, sophisticated young lady. She looked ridiculous.

She ran into the soddy, snatched her sunbonnet and extra gingham dress, and went inside the lean-to. She closed the sheet so no one could see her. Her hands trembled and her eyes filled with tears. She could hardly see as she fumbled with the endless row of pearl buttons on the princess dress.

"Addie?" Mother called.

Addie did not reply. She pitched Elizabeth's dress onto

103

the mattress and slipped into her own clothes. Staring in the mirror, she tried to smooth down the stiff, wild fringe on her forehead. Nothing seemed to control that bushy wad of hair. In desperation, she crammed on her sunbonnet and tied it tightly under her chin.

"Addie?" Mother called again. "You can't hide in there forever. Come out."

Addie wiped her face with her apron again.

"Don't take it so hard, Addie," Mother said. "Elizabeth didn't mean any harm. And your brothers, well, they just aren't used to you looking different—"

"Please, just leave me alone," Addie said bitterly. She hurried outside into the yard before Mother could embrace her and make her feel like a big, crying baby. She would never *look* like a capable, grown-up young lady. How could she ever hope to *be* one?

"Come back!" Mother called. "Don't run off, dear heart."

But Addie did not stop. She stumbled across the pasture, back to the creek. Her ankles buckled in the cursed, high-heeled boots. When she reached the protection of a group of trees, she yanked the laces and pitched Elizabeth's shoes into the grass. There! Now she could run barefoot, the way she knew best. Addie raced along the creek until she reached the secret place where the box elders and the cottonwoods shut out the big sky. She threw herself down onto the bank. Elizabeth had tricked her into believing she could look beautiful in her fancy dress and her fancy hairstyle. She had duped her into handing over the precious necklace. Worse yet, she had dazzled her into sending away her one, true friend. That was the cruelest trick of all. Addie cried and cried. She would never forgive Elizabeth. Never.

10 COUSIN OR ENEMY?

When she returned to the soddy, Addie found a piece of bread and butter Mother had left for her on the table. No one mentioned her red-rimmed eyes. No one, not even Elizabeth, mentioned the hairstyle or the outfit. Maybe it was because Mother had warned George and Burt to keep quiet. Or maybe it was because there were too many chores to be done. Elizabeth, who claimed the sun had given her a terrible headache, withdrew inside the lean-to. Her disappearance suited Addie just fine.

For the rest of the long, hot day, Addie and her brothers took turns raking the cut hay into rows called windrows. The work was nearly unbearable in the beating sun. Sweat bees stung Addie's bare arms. The bitter taste of dust filled her mouth. Brittle stems and bits of grass irritated her nose and eyes.

Sometimes she stopped to watch Pa and Ole. Pa was driving the mower. Ole sat atop the iron seat of the sweeper, driving the team of horses back and forth across the field of cut grass. The sweeper looked like a giant comb positioned between two wheels. It was a deadly piece of machinery. The twenty, razor-sharp, curved prongs pushed the windrows into bigger piles.

When the piles were ready, Pa and Ole would use two homemade buck rakes to pick them up and carry them to the stacks. A buck rake was a horse-drawn contraption with a dozen, long, metal-tipped teeth. When the buck rake arrived at a stack, the hay had to be pitched by hand into the growing stack.

George's job was to stand on top of each haystack and catch with a pitchfork the bunches thrown up to him by Pa and Ole. Each new bundle of grass had to be worked carefully in among the others so that the stack would not blow away in a strong wind. The middle was kept higher so that water could run off easily—"if it ever rains again," Pa said.

Because Addie's family had no stacking machine to lift and throw hay high into the air, their haystacks were never as tall as those of some neighbors. From a distance, the stacks reminded Addie of some giant's misplaced loaves of bread.

By late afternoon, they had finished their biggest stack. The air was as still and heavy as it had been for days. Even the birds had stopped singing.

Addie's arms and back ached. When she thought of how ridiculous Elizabeth had made her look that morning, she felt even more weary and defeated. She would never feel grown-up. What was she going to do about school? There was only one month before the letter was due to the Yankton Board of Examiners. It seemed impossible to make Mother understand that she was afraid to go. Maybe she could talk to Pa. Next time he came around with the mower, she called to him, "Can I ride a while?"

"What happened to your hair?"

She tucked a loose, frazzled strand inside her sunbonnet. "Nothing. It's just curled." She shifted uncomfortably on the seat. "Looks like a rut ahead," she said, to change the subject.

Hidden rises and the holes of foxes, skunks, and snakes could accidentally cripple the horses. Another danger was insects. It was not uncommon for a team tortured by the bites of horseflies to bolt madly across a field and overturn the rig. Pa had fastened a wire basket over each horse's sensitive nose for protection. But the team still seemed unusually skittish as it circled this last half-acre of standing grass.

Addie listened to the pleasant, steady *clat-ti-ka-clat-ti-ka* of the mower as they moved clockwise around the field. She liked the scent of the sweet, newly cut grass. She liked the orderly way the vibrating sickle bar fell, leaving a neat swath behind them.

What she didn't like was when the mower came upon a quail's nest or a frog that couldn't jump away fast enough. Although she took care to close her eyes tight, she could not avoid feeling the soft, jarring *chuck* when the deadly blade made a direct hit.

"Must be close to a hundred and ten degrees," Pa said. Underneath his wide-brimmed hat he wore a kerchief that he doused regularly with water that Mother brought out to the field. The water evaporated almost instantly, but it cooled him a little, and the kerchief helped keep the sun off his neck.

"I'd say it feels more like one hundred and thirty," Addie said.

"How are you and your cousins getting on?"

"All right, I guess," she lied. She felt too embarrassed to tell Pa how angry she was with Elizabeth.

"Elizabeth still won't come out and help us?"

"She's in the house. She says she has a headache."

Pa frowned. "Well, at least Maudie's willing to do her part. She's turning into a regular cook, isn't she? How'd you like the bread she made for dinner yesterday?"

"Better than the first batch. Remember how burned black and hard those loaves were? You could have used them to sharpen a plow."

Pa chuckled. "You bet."

Addie checked the horizon again. A soft wind was beginning to blow, as gently as someone letting out a deep breath. "Do you think it's going to storm?"

Pa rubbed the back of his knee, the one he claimed could forecast the weather. "Hard to say."

"Pa, do you have any idea when the cousins are going home?"

"I remember when you used to ask how long the cousins were going to *stay.*"

Addie squirmed. Having a visitor like Elizabeth was far worse than anything she had imagined.

"Elizabeth and Maudie never talk about how much they miss their parents. Don't you think they'd be getting lonesome to go home and see their folks?"

Pa shrugged. "Maybe they're just not the lonesome kind. Your mother wrote to Aunt Rachel saying the girls arrived safely. Mail is slow. I'm sure we'll get a letter one of these days telling us which train they'll be taking back to Sabula."

Addie could not detect much hope in Pa's voice. Was he worried, too, that their Iowa guests might never leave? Maudie was pleasant enough and always helped. But she seldom spoke or smiled. As for Elizabeth, she irked everyone in the family. Even Mother was becoming short-tempered with Elizabeth's increasing list of demands—a softer pillow, a specially cooked fried egg, a basin of fresh water at exactly the right temperature. The boys complained that flies pestered them at night when they had to sleep in the barn. Nellie accused Addie of taking all the space on the little cot. When would the cousins go back to Sabula so that life could be normal again?

On the far western edge of the horizon, faint light exploded. There was no rumble, no *whomp* of thunder. Just a mute, broken-glass glimmer. "Here she comes," Pa said. "Looks like heat lightning again. Never can tell if it's going to turn into the real thing or not. Just so we don't take any chances, I'm going to finish this last circle and then take the team in."

The worst place to be during a lightning storm was under a tree—or atop a mower or sweeper in the middle of a field. As usual, Addie knew her job would be to help keep a lookout for fires spawned by lightning. Sometimes it seemed to her as if she had spent the entire summer searching the horizon for fires and the sky for rain. So far, neither had materialized.

Addie cleared her throat. This might be her last chance in a very long while to speak to Pa alone. "You know, Pa, if this drought keeps up and we don't get much in the way of a harvest in the fall, maybe I should think about making other plans."

"Other plans?"

"You know, other school plans. Maybe I shouldn't be

going to Yankton. If times are tight, maybe you'll need me at home to help."

Pa shifted the reins to his other hand and sat up straight. "Times aren't going to be so tight for us as for other people. And I'm going to sell some of the replacement heifers."

"The replacement heifers? But that's your breeding stock. You always said a stockman ought to never sell the cattle that's supposed to take the place of the old cows."

"I didn't say I was going to sell all of them—just a few. Just the ones who are fatter and better-looking than their mothers. Don't you worry. Everything's going to be fine for you in the fall. You've got an excellent chance of winning that scholarship." Pa looked directly into her eyes. "It's a real opportunity. You might not have such a chance again."

Addie nodded.

How could she tell Pa she hadn't mailed the letter when he was making so many sacrifices for her? Her parents seemed so certain she'd succeed, but what if she took that test and failed? Mother and Pa would be too embarrassed to show their faces in town. Her brothers would laugh at her, the same way they had laughed when she wore Elizabeth's dress. She did not know what to do.

Cloud shadows raced across the prairie. A jagged bolt, like the leg of some giant, blue-white sky spider, plunged through the clouds to the ground. Addie held her breath— four, five, six, seven seconds. The ground shook as the thunder rumbled. "She's getting too close for me," Pa said. "You better go wave in Ole and the boys."

Addie jumped off the mower, her skirt billowing. About five miles away she saw something like a grey curtain pulling across the sky. A cool, brassy wind hurled slivers of grass into the air. The horses whinnied and rolled their eyes.

"Whoa! Now, whoa!" Pa called. "George is on that small stack. Tell him to help you warn the others. Watch for smoke. Remember, keep to the low places but don't go under any trees."

Addie watched Pa guide the team toward the barn. More than anything, she wanted to go back to the house where it was safe. But she knew she couldn't. She had to find her brother first. At the far end of the field, she spied Ole on the sweeper. He was hurrying toward the barn, too. His blue cap flew off, but he couldn't even stop for it. His team of spirited bays was too fast, too wild.

Another brilliant, crooked leg of the lightning spider danced along the ground. Thunder kicked and crashed. Instinctively, Addie ducked.

The storm was very close.

She hurried toward a distant, half-built stack. On top she could see a shape waving—George. He disappeared. He liked to leap off haystacks, in spite of Pa's warnings.

"George, where are Burt and Lew?" she shouted.

"At the house," he shouted back. Suddenly, the sky tore open with light. Addie put her hands to her ears, shut her eyes, and crouched on the ground, shaking. The hair on her arms and her head lifted. She could feel something buzzing and numbing in the air around her.

This time when she looked across the field, she spotted a strange glow.

"Addie!" George ran to her, pointing toward rising blue-black smoke. "A stack's been hit!"

As fast as they could, Addie and George sped back to the house, calling, "Pa! Mother! The big stack's burning!"

But their parents were already grabbing every available gunny sack and bucket. "Burt and Lew, you help your sister haul water. George, come with us," Pa barked. Ole rushed across the barnyard armed with three shovels.

Addie pumped pail after pail as Lew and Burt raced the water to the burning stack. There wasn't a moment to lose. The fire had to be put out before it spread. Addie's back ached as she pushed on the stiff pump handle. Sweat ran down her neck and arms.

"I'll pump now," Maudie volunteered. Addie picked

up a filled bucket that bruised her legs as she ran to the smoldering stack. Ole, George, Mother, and Pa doused sacks with water and beat the flames.

But nothing they did made any difference.

The lightning had hit the middle of the tinder-dry stack. There was no way to stop the burning deep inside. All they could do was prevent the fire from spreading. Pa and Ole dug a trench around the stack to act as a firebreak. They tossed dirt from the trench into the burning grass.

Maudie arrived with two sloshing buckets and a dipper. Her back was stained with sweat. Soot covered her cheeks and nose. Her hair and eyebrows were singed. "Here," she said hoarsely to Ole, offering him some water.

Ole bashfully bobbed his head. *'Tak.* I mean tank you very much kind lady."

Maudie smiled a timid grin, and for the first time, Addie noticed her fine white teeth.

Little by little, the thunder roared farther and farther away. Nothing else was hit by lightning, but the stack was a complete loss. Pa's face was streaked with black. Mother leaned on a shovel. Terrible disappointment flickered in their eyes. A whole stack—gone.

Thwock! The first hailstones rattled against the hard ground. There was a pause.

"We have to make a run for it," Mother shouted.

The wind picked up. Hailstones the size of pebbles pelted down harder and harder, stinging Addie's face and arms. "Come on, George!" she shouted, grabbing Lew and Burt by the hand. "Run!"

"How come we have to put up with lightning and thunder but all we get is hail?" George complained. "It isn't fair!"

The children raced across the field. By the time they reached the house, white, glistening hail covered the ground.

"Who left the door open?" Addie shouted, pushing her brothers inside. Slowly, her eyes became accustomed to the dim light.

"What in the—" George exclaimed.

"Oh, no," Addie whispered.

Something had happened, something awful.

Canned goods were tossed helter-skelter on the soddy floor. A bag of flour had been ripped apart, its white contents strewn under the table. The churn lay on its side. Lounging in a lake of butter was Miry. Kneeling next to him was Nellie May, who was patting a butter wig on his head and butter wings on his back. Miry licked his chops. His mouth, eyelashes, and chest were pale yellow. He had never looked happier.

Mother and Pa pushed between Addie and her brothers. "Nellie May!" Mother shouted in a shocked voice. "Miry!

Out! Get out of here!"

Miry made a greasy dash through everyone's legs and headed for the yard. For a few brief, horrible seconds, no one said anything.

"Nellie May!" Pa growled.

"McCoggy did it," Nellie said with a coy smile. She skated for a few seconds in the slick butter before Mother caught her and shook her hard.

"Where's Elizabeth? I told her to stay here and watch you."

"She got scared."

"Where did she go?" Pa demanded.

"I dunno. Out. She runned out."

Pa looked as furious as Addie had ever seen him. "Addie, I want you to go and check the barn and the root cellar. Find your cousin and bring her back to me. Now."

"Yes, sir," Addie said. What would Pa do? Would he spank Elizabeth? The idea seemed both frightening and fascinating.

Luckily, the hailstorm had ended. Addie hurried across the yard. She did not find Elizabeth hiding in the loft or among the cow stalls. She kicked small piles of icy pellets as she made her way to the root cellar. The cavernous cellar had its own small smokestack and wooden door that lifted on an angle. She pulled the heavy door open. "Elizabeth?" she called into the darkness.

"Well! It's about time somebody found me!" Elizabeth's piercing voice rang out. She wiped her face with her handkerchief as she stomped up the ladder. Her eyes flashed with anger. "Do you realize what it's like down there all alone in the dark? Why didn't anyone hear me calling? Why didn't anyone come?"

Addie did not reply. She could see Mother charging across the yard at full speed, wiping her greasy hands against her soot-covered apron. Behind her came Maudie, George, Lew, Burt, and Nellie May. "Elizabeth!" Mother shouted. "I told you to stay in the house with Nellie!"

"And where were you?" Elizabeth demanded, equally furious. "I was waiting and waiting down there. How could you leave me like that? How could you?"

"Fifty pounds of good butter is wasted because the pig got in the house!" Mother said angrily.

"Who cares about the butter? What about me? What if I had been hit by lightning?"

"You would have been perfectly safe if you had stayed in the house the way I told you. What about Nellie? What if she had wandered outside?"

"I don't know and I don't care. I'm not her nursery maid."

Pa stalked across the yard. He stood with his arms folded, staring at his niece. "Elizabeth," he said sternly, "it's time we had a talk."

Before Elizabeth could protest, Pa marched her into the barn. Addie gulped. Nellie hid her face in Addie's skirt. Her brothers exchanged terrified, amazed glances.

From out of the barn came a pitiful squealing.

A few minutes later, Elizabeth emerged, rubbing her back-side. When she discovered she still had an audience, she retreated to the soddy, head high, posture perfect. With a flourish, she slammed the door.

11 AN UNEASY PEACE

Early the next morning Addie awoke to the sound of squealing. Drowsily, she rubbed her eyes. What was happening? She climbed over her snoring sister and peeked around the sheet hanging over the lean-to doorway. Maudie and Elizabeth were still fast asleep. Addie pushed open the soddy door. She squinted in the bright sunlight, breathing in fresh air. Even though Mother and Maudie had spent two hours cleaning the night before, the greasy butter smell lingered indoors like the memory of a bad dream.

E-e-e-e-e-oink!

Miry! Addie hurried to the barnyard. Pa was leading the protesting pig up a plank into the back of the wagon. George, Lew, and Burt watched silently.

"Where are you taking Miry?" Addie asked. But already she knew. Her brothers' pale, mournful faces told her everything.

"Town," Pa replied. He did not look up as he tied the rope good and tight.

"The pig's got to be sold," Mother said gently. "You can see why, can't you?"

No, she could not. As the wagon rolled away, Addie put her hands to her ears to muffle Miry's pitiful cries. Grimly, George and Burt clenched their eyes shut. Lew, his face streaming with tears, bolted out of the barnyard and ran to the creek.

For three days, George, Lew, and Burt refused to speak to Elizabeth. Finally, she cornered Addie and the boys in the barn after milking. "What's the matter with all of you? I'd think you'd be glad to be rid of that vicious, filthy beast."

Addie grabbed Burt's arm before his flying fist could connect with Elizabeth's jaw. Elizabeth shielded herself with an empty bucket.

"You don't understand anything, do you?" George replied hotly. "Miry was our pet. He was practically a member of the family. He was sent away because of you, Princess Newtheenia."

"Don't you dare call me that name."

"I'll call you anything I want. You deserve worse."

"I don't care if she's a girl. Let me knock her head off!" Burt begged. Even though he barely came past Elizabeth's elbow, he struggled to give her a good punch.

"Stop it!" Addie shouted, fearful of what her brothers might do next. She had never seen them so angry.

"A bloody lip would look good on Princess Newtheenia," Burt snarled.

"Don't act so high and mighty, Addie," George said, rolling up his sleeves. "You hate her as much as we do."

Addie shrugged and let go of Burt's arm. George was right. She *did* hate Elizabeth. Because of her cousin, she had lost her best friend. She had lost her self-respect. She had lost Miry. Elizabeth deserved to be punched. But if something awful happened, Addie would surely be blamed. "Since you're the eldest, you're supposed to set a good example," Pa often reminded her.

"Aw, come on!" Burt complained. "What are we waiting for?" He took a step forward and drew back his fist.

This time it was Lew who interrupted. "Wait, I have a better idea. Let's make Elizabeth apologize."

"Apologize?" Burt said, disappointed.

"That's right. Apologize, Elizabeth. Right now."

Addie, George, and Burt stared dumbfounded at Lew. For once, why couldn't he break down and clobber somebody?

Elizabeth edged backward. "Why should I apologize?"

"Because of what you just called Miry," Lew said quietly.

"Aw, let me at least give her a bloody nose, Lew,"

Burt protested and rolled up his sleeves.

"And George and Burt," Lew continued, "you apologize for what you called Elizabeth."

The boys looked disgusted. "I don't know why my apology is necessary," Elizabeth said haughtily. "I was only telling the truth about that...that animal. But if saying I'm sorry will stop this life-threatening situation, all right, I'll do it. I apologize."

George's eyes narrowed.

"Come on, George and Burt," Lew insisted. "She said it. Now it's your turn."

Grudgingly, the boys mumbled, "Sorry." They scrambled up the ladder to the loft. Elizabeth slipped through the barn door without another word.

Addie stared at Lew in bewilderment. "Why?" she whispered. "Why did you stop them just now?"

Lew's bony shoulders straightened. "Miry was the smartest, handsomest, kindest pig," he said slowly. "All his life he never hurt anyone on purpose. It just didn't seem right fighting about him like that. He wouldn't have wanted it. I know he wouldn't."

When Addie put her hand on Lew's shoulder, he shrugged free. "I don't want to talk about it anymore."

The days dragged by, hot and endless. Addie and her brothers helped finish the haying and did their regular chores. Maudie lent a hand with the milking and cooking.

Only when all her work was finished did she disappear with one of the books Addie had lent her, *Robinson Crusoe* or *Gulliver's Travels*. Not once did Addie see Maudie or Elizabeth write a letter home. Not once did they receive a letter from Aunt Rachel.

Moodily, Elizabeth helped with dishes, swept the floor, and churned butter. She never volunteered to do more. She did not talk to anyone. Her only companion was her doll, Jessica, who accompanied her on long afternoon escapes to Rattling Creek.

It was, at best, an uneasy peace. Addie and her brothers avoided Elizabeth as much as possible, a difficult feat in a small house with so little privacy.

July came. Heat hammered the land worse than ever. When Addie closed her eyes at night, even the inside of her eyelids held the memory of the sun's brightness.

The only clouds in the sky were pale smudges, floating past like gasping fish. Even the boys' dream of tracking the famous outlaw parched and died. What was the point? Everyone went about their chores without laughing, without speaking, almost without thinking. It was just too hot to do more.

By mid-July, the ground began to crack and split apart. Powder-fine dust settled on the soddy's plank floor, on the table, on everything. Mother kept the clean dishes turned upside down to keep out the dirt. But Addie could still feel the grit in her teeth.

Dawn was the coolest time of the day. One morning, very early, before her brothers awoke, Addie crept silently out to the barn. "Two weeks," she thought miserably. "Just two weeks until the first of August." She opened the cigar box. For the hundredth time, she reread the letter from the Yankton Board of Examiners. *August first...August first.* She put the letter back and snapped the box shut.

Addie filled the bucket at the pump, then watered Mother's shade trees and the vegetable garden. The tomato vines and bean plants had never recovered from the hailstorm. She concentrated on sprinkling the surviving parsnips, carrots, and potatoes hidden underground. What would be left to eat when winter came?

Nothing around her looked the way she remembered it had other summers. Cottonwoods, turned prematurely yellow, rattled in the wind. Curled corn leaves were lined with brown. Flax, which by now should have been blue as a rippling lake, lay wilted and scorched. Oat heads had cooked and shriveled in the hot sun until the grain was as light as chaff.

The grass was haggard and grey. Every swale, every hill, every rise and crease in the land showed through, like ribs on a skinny heifer. Knife-sharp stubble cut Addie's bare feet as she went out to the night pasture to bring in the cows. The herd, foraging for what few green blades could be found along the creek fence, moved slowly, panting. When their hungry bawling began, Addie pressed her hands to her ears. She could not bear to hear the lowing of the calves, who followed their mothers. The young cows' heads drooped, and foam clung to their mouths.

Once inside the barnyard, the cattle hurried to the stock tank. At least the water from the pump still ran fresh. The water in Rattling Creek was low and warm, and it moved sluggishly. Worse yet, Addie's secret place was clogged with foul-smelling moss and slime.

Only the sinkhole seemed unaffected by the drought. Instead of drying up, the muck there seemed more treacherous than ever. Addie was careful to keep the cows away from the spot. A week earlier, two cows, desperate for a drink, had mistakenly wandered across the sinkhole and become trapped. Pa had had to tie ropes to two of his strongest horses to pull them out.

Addie gazed at the morning sky. Still no sign of rain. But what could be done? Nothing. Nothing except watch and wait. For the past week, there had been no field work. The crops were too fragile to cultivate. In such drought, even weeds could not grow.

"Morning, Addie," Pa said as he trudged out of the house. He bent over and picked up a clump of soil. The dirt shattered in his fist. He scanned the horizon and shook his head. "Never seen weather like this. Six whole weeks without a drop of rain."

"You want me to tell Mother you'll be eating breakfast with us?" Addie asked.

"Too hot to eat," Pa replied, his voice impatient. Idleness made him high-strung and irritable. In spite of the drought, he seemed determined to keep busy. "I'm going out to plow a fire guard around the haystack in the south bog. Yesterday I saw the tenth family this week on the road heading east. Told me their well went dry."

"Our well water's still coming up fine, Pa," Addie said, trying to sound cheerful.

"Seems the rattlers know it, too. You best be careful. Around sunset I saw a snake coiled up near the pump, bold as you please. Guess that rattler had as much right as the rest of us to feel thirsty."

"Guess so." Addie smiled. It seemed ever so long since she had heard Pa make a joke. Even a little joke.

"Did Mother tell you about the surprise?"

"What surprise?" Addie asked.

"You're going to pick plums down by the Jim River today. It's all arranged. You and Mother and the cousins are going to take Lew, Burt, and Nellie. George is going to stay here with me to watch for fires."

"But Pa, the Jim is twelve miles from here. How are

we going to do much plumming before nightfall?"

"You're going to stay overnight—camp under the stars. It's your mother's idea. It will be cooler there, and we certainly will be needing all the fruit we can preserve this year."

"But what about Elizabeth? What about Maudie? What if they don't like to camp out under the stars?"

"Well, there's only one way to find out, isn't there? By the way, your mother told Ole to invite Tilla. I'm sure her family can use some plums, too."

"Tilla?" She hadn't seen Tilla in such a long time. "Did Tilla...did she say she'd go with us?"

Pa nodded. "Ole's bringing her this morning when he comes for his pay. You better get busy and help Mother pack the wagon."

As she carried bedding and baskets out to the wagon, Addie did not feel the heat. A trip! She could hardly wait. In only a few hours, she would be leaving behind all the chores of the farm. Better yet, Tilla would be coming, too. Maybe this was Addie's chance to set things right.

Mother packed three kerosene lamps, a canvas tarp, a coffee pot, a kettle, tin plates, and cups. Their food supplies included a bag of cornmeal, cold biscuits, several loaves of bread, a big wedge of cheese, a slab of bacon, a bag of beans, raw carrots, hard-boiled eggs, and a jug of fresh water.

For a change, Elizabeth seemed enthusiastic. She packed her own carpet bag. "Toiletries and other essential items of civilization," she told Addie. "Soap, perfume, lavender water, lotion, and talcum powder."

Addie smirked. "Have you ever camped out before?"

"Of course not! My family always travels first class. We only stay in the very best hotels."

Maudie stuffed a pair of work gloves into a small satchel filled with a change of clothing and an extra pair of shoes. She also took along her black parasol. "In case it rains," she explained.

"Addie!" Mother called. "Tilla's coming!"

Addie held her breath as she watched Tilla cross the yard. Would she still be angry with her?

"Hello, Tilla!" Mother said.

Tilla nodded a shy greeting. Her arms were filled with a stack of bushel baskets and gunnysacks. She carried no extra clothing.

"Is that everything, Tilla?" Mother asked, as Pa lifted the last of the supplies into the wagon.

"Yes. Only oder ting I brought vas dis." She opened her hand. Inside her palm was a smooth, white rock. "I find it on de vay here."

"Very pretty," Addie said. "You've got a good eye for finding things."

Tilla grinned. "Any time you velcome to borrow it."

Now it was Addie's turn to smile.

"Climb aboard everyone," Mother said. "There's not much space, but I'm sure we'll manage."

Mother and Maudie sat on the wagon seat. Addie, Nellie May, Burt, and Lew squeezed in back with Elizabeth and Tilla. But in spite of the cramped quarters, Addie was delighted. She and Tilla had patched their quarrel. They were best friends again. The only thing that marred their departure was George, who looked very sullen as he waved goodbye. Last year, George could have gone plumming. Now he was too old. He had to stay and help Pa.

"Goodbye, George!" Nellie May screamed. Addie had to hold her dress so she would not fall out. Mother rattled the reins, and the horses started off toward the Jim River.

As the wagon rocked and lurched along, a cloud of dust puffed up. Tilla settled in between Addie and Elizabeth.

"Well, won't this be fun! A real adventure," Elizabeth said, beaming in Tilla's direction.

Addie glanced suspiciously at her cousin. Elizabeth did not seem one bit like her usual glum self. And she was acting very chatty and friendly toward Tilla. Had she forgotten she had said Tilla was crude and ignorant?

"I love to travel, don't you, Tilla?" Elizabeth continued. "That's your name, isn't it?"

Tilla nodded shyly.

"How unusual. Is that your *real* name?"

Tilla looked confused. "I am also called 'Mathilde' but not so much."

Elizabeth smiled. "Tilla, you want to know what my favorite word is?"

"Vat?"

"My favorite word is *numinous.*"

Addie rolled her eyes. Of course Elizabeth would pick a word that nobody else possibly understood.

"Vat is...*numinous?*" Tilla asked.

"*Numinous* describes me, actually," Elizabeth said with a toss of her curls. "Take a guess."

Tilla shook her head.

"Oh, come, come. Give it a try."

"Numinous means you like to talk maybe?"

Elizabeth laughed. "No. It means 'awe-inspiring, filled with fascination and compelling mystery'."

Tilla smiled politely, while Addie made a disgusted face.

"Would you like to see my doll?" Elizabeth whispered to Tilla, loud enough so that Addie could hear. She opened her carpet bag and took out Jessica.

"Oh!" Tilla gasped.

Elizabeth pushed the blinking blonde doll into Tilla's arms. "Here. I'll let her ride in your lap the whole trip.

I don't mind. I'm very generous. I like to share my things with people. Especially people like you."

"Like...like me?"

"Yes, you seem to be a very sensitive human being. I think you and I will be great friends."

"You do?"

Elizabeth flashed a numinous smile. Addie tried not to look. She tried not to listen. The other two girls were ignoring her completely. How could they be so mean? "I'm going to walk for a while," Addie announced. "Do you want to come, Tilla?" Maybe Tilla would walk with her and they could be alone, and she could at last tell someone all about Elizabeth's selfishness.

But Tilla did not budge. She clutched Jessica and nodded every now and then as Elizabeth talked. Why, Tilla had not even heard a word Addie had said!

Addie jumped off the back of the moving wagon and landed in a dusty heap. She stood up and brushed herself off casually, as if she had meant to land that way. When she glanced up, Elizabeth and Tilla were whispering together and laughing. Were they laughing at her?

"Addie?" Mother called. "You have to tell me when you're jumping off like that. Are you going to walk? It's a long way to the Jim River."

"Yes, Mother," Addie replied. She didn't care how long it was. She didn't want to sit next to Tilla and Elizabeth and listen to them whisper about her. She didn't want to hear them at all. She'd walk as slowly as she could, a long way behind the wagon, following the tracks in the dirt.

By the time Mother had stopped for lunch, Addie was hot, tired, and footsore. She hobbled to the shady spot where Maudie was spreading an old blanket underneath a tree.

"There you are, Addie," Maudie said. "Why don't you sit down and rest?"

Addie shook her head. Burt and Lew and Nellie raced past in a game of tag. "Where's Tilla? Where's Elizabeth?"

"Still chatting away," Maudie said, slicing a loaf of bread. "They seem to be getting along. I'm so glad Aunty Becca invited Tilla. She seems to make my sister happy."

Addie sniffed. What did she care about Elizabeth's happiness?

"Here they come," Maudie said, pointing.

As the girls came closer, arm in arm, Addie saw something around Tilla's neck. Why, it was *her* Indian necklace! "You two seem to be great friends," she said curtly.

Tilla blushed. "Elizabeth gif me de necklace."

Addie glared at Elizabeth. "How dare you? That necklace belongs to me!"

Elizabeth sniffed. "It's mine now. I can do with

134

it whatever I wish."

"Look here, girls," Mother interrupted. "Ripe buffalo berries. Right here in these bushes." She pointed to dark orange berries. "If we're careful of the thorns, we can pick quite a few, maybe enough to make jelly when we get home. What's the matter, Addie?"

"Nothing," Addie replied. She wished she had never agreed to this trip. Most of all, she wished Elizabeth had never left Sabula.

"I'm going to help Maudie unpack the rest of the lunch. You girls come and sit down in a minute, all right?"

"Yes, Mother," Addie said.

"Before we eat, you want me to tell your fortune, Elizabeth?" Burt asked.

"Go ahead, it won't hurt," Lew replied, smiling.

This was the first time the boys had initiated a conversation with Elizabeth since Miry was sent away. Addie wondered what they were up to.

"It will only take a moment, really," Burt promised. "Just give me your hand."

"You're not scared are you?" Addie asked.

"Of course not." She calmly thrust out her hand, palm up.

Burt examined it carefully. He traced the lines of her palm with his finger. "I see here that when you grow up you will have a large mansion."

"Where do you see that?" Elizabeth asked excitedly.

"Right here," Burt replied, pointing to a squiggly wrinkle.

"What else do you see?"

"Here, I see a carriage with a team of fine horses."

Elizabeth grinned at Tilla. "You see, I'll be rich. I knew it. I knew I would be rich."

"And now, let me look closer," Burt continued. "Yes...I cannot be sure, but...do you wish to live by the sea?"

"A mansion by the sea?" Elizabeth gushed. "That sounds wonderful. Where do you see the sea?"

"*Right here!*" he said, spitting into Elizabeth's palm. In a flash, he and Lew ran away. Addie and Tilla looked at each other and giggled.

Furiously, Elizabeth wiped her hand in the grass. "Don't you two dare laugh at me! Aunty Becca!" she wailed, and ran to Mother.

12 TRUTH FOR TRUTH

The Jim River stretched about one hundred fifty yards wide, twice the size of Rattling Creek. The water was deep green, and the banks were covered with a sticky clay. On both sides stood more trees than Addie had seen in a very long time. In the late afternoon shade, long branches dipped into the rippling water.

As soon as Mother stopped the wagon, Addie turned to Tilla and whispered, "Come on. Let's go exploring!"

It was very satisfying to leave Elizabeth, who sat pouting. She had refused to speak to anyone since the spitting incident. Addie was glad to be getting back at her sly cousin. Elizabeth could stay in the wagon until she rotted!

Tilla and Addie wandered beneath a whispering grove of soft maples, box elders, and gnarled oaks.

"It's as quiet here as the bottom of a well, isn't it?" Addie said in a hushed voice.

Tilla nodded. "Your cousin, she has lots of ideas. You had many good times in your club?"

Addie sighed and shook her head. "Elizabeth...well, her visit hasn't worked out the way I expected."

"Cousins who stay too long, dey are all de same. Much trouble."

Unlike Elizabeth, who was tricky and sly, Tilla always said exactly what was on her mind.

"You are still my very best friend in de whole vorld, Addie. Am I right?"

Addie nodded.

"I got someting dat belong to you." Tilla handed her the Indian necklace. "I don't feel right to keep it."

Addie smiled. "Thanks." She slipped the necklace around her own neck, glad to have her eagle feather back at last.

The girls walked along the river. The water looked as if it might be lower than usual. Roots which ordinarily were underwater lay exposed, covered with dried strands of moss and dead plants. In some places the ground was marshy, and in the soft mud were the elegant, two-toed footprints of deer. Something else caught Addie's eye. She bent closer. Heel marks from a man's boot.

"Look at me, Addie!" Burt cried.

She stood up in time to see her brother wade out into a bubbly, sandy area. He waved. Suddenly, his look of pleasure changed to panic.

"I'm sinking! Help!" Burt cried.

For a moment, Addie did not know what to do. If she told her brother he was in quicksand, he would struggle and sink even faster. She had seen Pa rescue cattle from the sinkhole. She'd have to remember what he had done.

"Hold still, Burt!" Addie shouted, running to him.

"Grab a branch!" Tilla shouted.

Addie picked up a stick and held it out. Burt grabbed hold. Hand over hand, Addie hauled in her brother.

Burt staggered onto solid ground. He looked back at the mysterious spot that had nearly been his undoing. The water swirled, murky as thick pea soup. "That wasn't so scary. I was only sunk to this part of my leg," Burt boasted, pointing to his calves.

"Vat's dat on you?" Tilla asked. "Someting from de quicksand?"

"That was quicksand?" Burt's manly expression evaporated. He looked down at his legs. Suddenly, tears welled up in his eyes. "A leech! Get it off me, Addie! Get it off!"

"Hold still now. It'll be all right." Addie tried to be calm. Although she had removed plenty of leeches after wading in Rattling Creek, she still thought they were disgusting. Gingerly, she grasped the slimy, black creature and pulled gently. The inch-long leech stretched as if it were made of rubber before it loosened its grip and rolled to the ground.

The children were all very hot, but after that no one wanted to wade in the Jim. Picking wild plums didn't seem to be such a horrible way to spend the afternoon.

They carried baskets and crates and wandered among the thick wild plum bushes. They easily pulled away the fragrant red and yellow fruit. With plenty of water from the Jim, the plums grew easily, unaffected by the drought. Picking plums, Addie decided, was a far sight easier than haying. The air was almost cool along the river, and the birds sang. Out of the corner of her eye, she watched Elizabeth moving alone among the plum bushes. Addie touched the eagle feather. How Elizabeth had sulked when she saw the necklace around Addie's neck again!

For dinner, Mother fried salt pork with thin slices of some wild turnip she had discovered along the bluffs surrounding the river on both sides. The tired plum pickers sat around the bright campfire with their plates in their laps. "Just like cowboys," Lew said, grinning.

Because for once there was plenty of wood, they burned pieces of dry maple and burr oak. Addie sniffed the air. She had nearly forgotten the pleasing scent of wood smoke—so different from the harsh smell of burning coal or cow chips or twisted grass, the fuel they ordinarily had to use.

Nellie poked a long stick into the fire and held the shining tip aloft. She waved the stick in the air and sparks flew, as bright as the stars beginning to show in the evening sky.

"Careful, Nellie," Mother cautioned.

"She's trying to write her name with light, aren't you, Nellie?" Maudie said, smiling.

Nellie nodded. "McCoggy makes his name, too," she said. Her face was smeared with dirt and plum juice, but she looked quite pleased with herself.

Addie wished Pa and George could have been there to see how many buckets and baskets of plums they had picked. In the morning, there would be time to pick even more.

Elizabeth threw handfuls of dry twigs into the fire and watched them burn. "Aunty Becca," she said, finally breaking her long silence, "where are we supposed to sleep tonight? Did you bring a tent?"

"No, we don't have a tent. We'll just sleep on the ground or in the wagon," Mother replied.

"Oh," said Elizabeth, "on the ground? What about spiders and snakes? And what about the wild animals roaming around in the dark?"

Addie enjoyed seeing how miserable Elizabeth looked. Addie did not feel afraid. She had slept under the open sky before. Besides, she had her sister, her brothers, her mother, her cousins, and her best friend with her.

"Don't worry, Elizabeth," Mother reassured her. "We'll keep a fire burning. Animals are afraid to come too close to a fire. We'll be perfectly safe, I promise you."

"Anybody know any good ghost stories?" Burt asked.

"You all think you can scare me, don't you?" Elizabeth suddenly snapped. "Well, I'm not scared. I'm not scared a bit."

"Now, now, Elizabeth," Maudie said quietly. "Burt didn't mean any harm. He was just joking."

"Just the way he was joking when he told my fortune." Elizabeth glared at Addie, then her eyes darted from the necklace to Tilla. "I know you all hate me."

"No one hates you," Mother said. "I think you're just tired from the long day. Perhaps we should all turn in now and get a good night's rest."

Elizabeth crossed her arms defiantly. "I'm not the least bit tired. I'm not going to sleep."

No one said anything. The peaceful atmosphere had been ruined. Lew and Burt got up, ready to spread out the blankets.

Mother motioned for them to sit down. "I suppose we can sit here a little longer. What would you like to talk about?"

No one spoke. Elizabeth scowled into the fire.

Mother seemed determined to brighten her niece's

spirits. "Let's talk about school. That's something you all know well."

"School's over," Burt complained. "It's summer. I like summer because there's no school. Why do we have to talk about it?"

"Vell, I vant to talk about it. I love school," Tilla said with enthusiasm. "And ven Addie goes to high school in Yankton, I am going to visit her on de train all by myself."

Addie looked down and hugged her knees. Not high school again! Couldn't Tilla think of something else to talk about?

"That's a wonderful idea, Tilla," Mother said.

Addie yawned dramatically. "I'm really very tired. I think I might turn in now—"

"And ven I come to Yankton to visit Addie, ve might go to a restaurant ver dey haf dose pieces of paper. Vat you call dem?"

"Menus?" Maudie asked helpfully.

"Menus! Ya, dat's it. You look at de menu and you pick vat you eat." Tilla gazed happily into the fire. "I order chocolate ice cream for sure."

"It's all very well and good to dream about going to Yankton, but let's be realistic, shall we?" Elizabeth said, smiling.

Addie squirmed. "I don't think anyone's interested in

hearing about—"

"I happen to know for a fact," Elizabeth continued in her ringing voice, "that it's impossible for Addie to go to high school."

Mother leaned forward. "Whatever are you saying, Elizabeth? Addie is taking the scholarship test in the fall. When she wins that scholarship, which I'm sure she will, she'll go to Yankton just the way Tilla said. Isn't that right, Addie?"

Addie didn't answer. She stared into the fire.

"If my memory serves me correctly," Elizabeth went on, "—and I do have a nearly perfect memory, don't I, Maudie?—there was a certain paragraph in a certain letter that said, 'If you would be so kind as to return this signed document post-haste to the Board of Examiners, Yankton, you will be eligible to take the high school scholarship examination. Please be advised that the deadline to receive your reply is August first. If we do not hear from you by then, you will no longer be considered a candidate.' If I'm not mistaken, August first is just fifteen days away."

Addie clenched her teeth. How could her cousin be so sneaking and low-down? She hated Elizabeth more than she had ever hated anyone in her life.

"How do you know what that letter said, Elizabeth?" Mother asked.

Elizabeth took a deep dramatic breath. "Because I

know how to follow people very cleverly so that they don't suspect a thing. And I've watched Addie take that letter from the box in the barn and read it. When she wasn't looking, I read it myself."

"In the barn? It can't be. Addie sent that letter back to Yankton months ago. Didn't you, Addie?" Mother asked, her voice quavering. "Didn't you?"

Slowly, miserably, Addie shook her head. She could not even look at Mother. She felt too ashamed.

"You did not send it?" Tilla whispered in disbelief.

"So you see," Elizabeth announced triumphantly, "the truth is known. Addie is a liar."

The fire spit and sparks rose. Maudie stood up. "Elizabeth!" she said, louder than anyone had ever heard her speak before. "Don't you know when to stop?"

Elizabeth glared at her sister. "Sit down and be quiet, Maudie."

"I will not sit down and be quiet," Maudie replied. "If you're going to be so free with other people's secrets, I think you should be free with your own, too."

Elizabeth shrugged, as if she had no idea what Maudie was talking about.

"There are certain secrets that my sister and I share, don't we, Elizabeth? Secrets about why we're here, for instance."

"Now girls, really," Mother tried to interrupt.

But Maudie would not be stopped. "Your whole family has been so generous to us. Right from the start we should have told you why we came, but we didn't. We couldn't. I kept waiting for Mother to write and let you know. But she never did. I have to tell you the truth. I simply must. It all started about eight months ago."

"Maudie," Elizabeth warned, "*don't.*"

"Eight months ago," Maudie began again, "Father disappeared. He left us to go west to prospect. That's what he said. The real reason, we later discovered, was that he was bankrupt and could never show his face in Sabula again. Father's creditors from his various unscrupulous business dealings arrived and began dismantling our house. We were evicted—thrown out in the street—and disgraced in front of our relatives and neighbors."

"Stop!" Elizabeth said, her hands over her ears.

Maudie did not pay any attention to her sister. "Mother was beside herself. She is a very proud woman. Too proud for us to stay with Grandpa, who has disapproved of Father from the beginning. She packed us up with whatever of her fine possessions she had hidden and sent us to you. Fortunately, you didn't think of turning us away."

Mother looked stunned. "I can't believe it."

"I have no idea where Mother is," Maudie continued. "She said she would write to us as soon as she found a place to live."

"So that's why you and Elizabeth had all that silver tableware and candlesticks in your trunks," Mother said slowly.

Maudie nodded. "All we own now is what we brought. Elizabeth and I are completely penniless. We have been sent away to be kept out of the way. Isn't that right, Elizabeth? The fine house and fine furniture and fine, loving parents—all gone for good."

Elizabeth was on her feet, her eyes flashing. "Shut up, Maudie! Shut up, right this minute!"

"I will *not* shut up," Maudie replied, her voice trembling. "I'm telling them the truth. I don't care how unpleasant it sounds. There is nothing left for us back in Sabula. Nothing. And you might as well get used to the idea."

Without a word, Elizabeth bolted from the firelight and fled into the shadows.

"Elizabeth!" Mother shouted. "Where are you going? Come back!"

But Elizabeth had already disappeared.

13 ADDIE'S SEARCH

For a long time Addie gazed numbly into the darkness after Elizabeth. At last she turned to her mother. "I can explain everything, if you'll just let me."

"Can we talk about it when we get home, Addie?" Mother sounded weary. "I just wish you'd told me and Pa what you'd done. Now we've got to rethink this thing. And right now, after hearing what Maudie had to say, I'm not thinking so clearly." Mother sighed. "Poor, proud Rachel! She must have nearly died of shame."

Mother stared into the fire. "Funny thing about being away from home for three years," she continued softly, "you forget what might really be happening. You forget that there might be sorrows because all that you're remembering and pining for are the good times and the happy people you're afraid you'll never see again."

"What should we do about Elizabeth?" Addie asked timidly.

"Ya. You tink maybe ve should go get her?" Tilla asked.

"I think we should leave my sister alone," Maudie said. "She needs to think about things by herself for a little while."

Burt and Lew moved closer to Nellie, who sat between them on a log. The younger children anxiously watched Mother's every move. What did all this mean? What was going to happen?

"Maudie," Mother said quietly, "I'm so sorry. If I had only known..." She reached out to caress Maudie, but Maudie shrank away.

"You have been much kinder to us than we deserved," Maudie murmured. She sat down, put her face in her big hands, and wept. Mother patted Maudie's bent head.

Addie shivered. The whole world seemed as if it had turned upside down. What would it be like to discover that her own father was a thief? How would *she* feel if she found out that Pa had deserted the family? Addie tried to imagine losing her home and being sent away, not knowing where her mother was or when she would ever hear from her again. She felt so sorry for Maudie. And to her surprise, she even felt sorry for Elizabeth.

A half-hour passed. Maudie had stopped crying; she helped Tilla and Addie arrange blankets on the ground for the younger children. The boys curled up in their bed and fell asleep. Mother rocked Nellie in her arms and then lowered her quietly to a quilt. Still, there was no sign of Elizabeth. "Maudie," Mother asked, "don't you think she should be back by now?"

"She doesn't usually stay mad this long," Maudie agreed. "She comes back pretty quickly after she flies off in one of her rages. She's never liked the dark, ever since she was little."

Addie thought about the crying she had heard the first night the cousins came. It had been Elizabeth after all.

"Vat if she get lost, fall in de vater, and drown?" Tilla said.

Addie flinched. Why did Tilla always have to be so blunt?

"I'm sure she wouldn't be foolish enough to try to cross the river," Mother said. "But we must go look for her."

Addie thought about the bluffs and trees along the Jim. Beyond the river, the prairie was pitch dark and wild. Elizabeth had no idea where she was. She could wander off and be lost for days.

"Addie, you, Maudie, Tilla, and I will search. I'll wake Burt and Lew. They can stay here and keep an eye on Nellie. Each of you carry a lantern. I'll take a torch. Addie, you go north along the river. Tilla, you go south. Maudie, you head northwest and I'll go southwest. Try and stay within sight of our campfire. If you find Elizabeth, come back to camp and bang on this big frying pan."

Addie started north, following the river. She held the lantern high to make a wide circle of light. Somehow the circle made her feel safer.

"Elizabeth! Elizabeth!" she called. She could hear the low rumble of the sluggish current and smell the musty river. "Don't go near the water," she said under her breath. She thought of the rhyme Elizabeth had recited on that day so long ago when they had formed the Wet Rat Club.

Mother, may I go out to swim?
Yes, my darling daughter.
Hang your clothes on a hickory limb
And don't go near the water.

What was that? She stopped and held perfectly still. A sound—was something following her? Her heart raced. She listened, but the noise faded away. Just some animal in the underbrush. Maybe a beaver or a deer.

"Elizabeth, where are you?" Addie called. The light bobbed in her trembling hand. She moved a few more feet and stopped. There it was again—footsteps! Who was following her? Frantically, she hurried forward into the darkness. She tripped but did not drop the lantern. She groped over roots, through willows. Her dress caught on something and ripped. A branch snapped back and cut her face. "Elizabeth! Answer me!"

Something large bumped her shoulder. Addie screamed and reached out. A tree—it was only a tree. She slumped against the rough bark and tried to calm herself.

"Addie? Addie?" That familiar voice!

"Elizabeth!" Addie shouted.

"Come quick!"

"Keep calling—I'm coming!" Addie hurried farther upstream, following the sound of her cousin's voice. She climbed around a tangle of fallen trees and stopped. Below her stretched a muddy embankment that sloped a foot before it met the current. "Elizabeth?"

"Help!"

Addie lifted her lantern and peered out over the river. She gasped. There was Elizabeth's ghostly shape. The water was almost up to her waist. She waved her arms. "I tried to cross, but now I'm sinking! I can't move my legs. Help me, Addie!"

The quicksand!

Addie's mind raced. What should she do? If she ran back for help, it might be too late. She had to do something now, by herself.

"Don't panic! If you move around too much, you'll only make things worse," Addie said.

"Please help me," Elizabeth begged, her voice small and faraway.

Addie found a nearby tree branch and hooked the lantern onto it. Then she held another branch with one hand and reached for Elizabeth's outstretched hand. Not close enough.

Addie tried again. Elizabeth grabbed for her hand, missed, and plunged face first.

"Elizabeth!" Addie screamed.

Elizabeth thrashed in the water, struggling to get her head above the current. She coughed and stood upright. Now the water came just past her waist.

"Try and stay calm," Addie warned.

"Calm! How can I? I'm caught to my knees!"

Addie tried to think. If only she had a piece of rope. If only she had a belt—anything to throw. What about her apron? She untied it from her waist and twisted the entire thing into a kind of rope, knotted at one end. She threw that end out to Elizabeth.

Elizabeth missed again.

Addie clutched the willow branch. This time she would lean out and throw the apron at the same moment. "Get ready!" she cried. But just as she threw, she thought about dark, squirming leeches down in the water. Her hand jerked, and the apron fell short of its mark.

"I'm going to die here," Elizabeth said, sobbing. "I

know it. I'm so miserable and I'm going to die."

"Shut up, Elizabeth. Stop crying and help me."

Elizabeth whimpered. Now the water was nearly to her armpits.

Addie tried not to panic. By now the quicksand must be all the way to Elizabeth's thighs. How would she ever be able to pull her out? She musn't think about that. She must concentrate on only one thing—throwing as far and as accurately as she could. "Are you ready this time? This time we're going to do it, I know. Now hold out your hand, Elizabeth."

Addie leaned. The twisted apron sailed through the air.

Elizabeth lunged. She caught the tip, dropped it, and began to wail loudly.

"Don't give up now, Elizabeth." Addie's hands were slippery with sweat. She glanced back into the darkness. Maybe the others would come; maybe they had heard her and they would come and help. "You have a loud voice. We can call Maudie and Mother together."

"It's too late," Elizabeth said mournfully. "Before I die, I want to say I'm really sorry for reading your letter and telling your mother. I really am. Will you forgive me? Please, say you will, so I can go to heaven."

"Of course I forgive you," Addie said impatiently. "Now hold out your hand again. Try hard. Are you listening?

You have to help me if you're going to save yourself."

Addie gripped the willow branch with all her might. There was always the danger that she might lose her balance and land in the quicksand herself. But this time, she was going to really stretch. She was going to throw the end of the apron with all her strength. "Are you ready?" She took a deep breath.

She leaned out and flung the apron. Her hand slipped from the willow.

In that split second, someone grabbed her wrist with an iron grip. Addie lunged toward Elizabeth—just enough for her to finally make the catch. With both hands, Elizabeth clutched the apron. Addie felt as if she were stretching...stretching like a leech.

"Maudie?" Addie said hoarsely. "Pull us in!" But when she turned, she caught sight of the hand that held her own so tightly.

It was not Maudie's.

It was a massive, hairy hand, a man's hand. And around his wrist jangled a chain and metal bracelet—the remains of a sawed-off handcuff.

14   A NUMINOUS SMILE

Addie could not even scream—Elizabeth might let go. She felt the stranger's strong arms around her waist. Now she could use both hands to grip the apron and pull her cousin to safety. "Come on, Elizabeth. You're doing just fine." Her knees shook. Sweat poured down the sleeves of her dress. Her shoulders ached. How much longer would the sash hold? "Don't let go!"

The quicksand made a loud sucking noise as Elizabeth struggled toward shore. The stranger took a step backward, as if he were digging in with his feet. He tugged. Addie winced but did not cry out. She focused on Elizabeth and forced herself to not look back.

"I don't think...I don't think I can do it," Elizabeth whined.

"You can! Don't give up, now! Come on, come on!"

Elizabeth stumbled and splashed.

"Don't let go!" Addie shouted. She pulled as if she

were hauling a stoneboat over rough ground. Elizabeth inched closer...closer still. She reached and grasped Addie's hands. With all her remaining strength, Addie hoisted her to the bank. Elizabeth crawled ashore and collapsed.

At that moment, the man let go. Addie stumbled and fell to her knees, breathing in great gulps. When she looked up, she expected to see a menacing figure towering over her. Instead, she saw nothing. He was gone.

"Come back!" Addie called softly, although she did not really mean it.

"Who are you talking to?" Elizabeth whispered.

"Didn't you see him?"

"See who?"

Addie strained to hear footsteps. But the night was quiet. The trembling in her knees stopped. She felt strangely calm. But what should she do? If she tried to explain exactly how she had managed to save her, Elizabeth would surely tell Mother. And then what? Mother would tell the Defiance sheriff, and the outlaw would be tracked down and caught by the Vigilance Committee. After what the stranger had done for Elizabeth, could Addie send him to the gallows? No—not even for a thousand-dollar reward.

"Tell me. Who's there?" Elizabeth whispered again.

Addie let out her breath slowly. "No one. I guess it was just my imagination. Do you think you can stand up?"

"Maybe. I don't know. My legs are shaking pretty badly."

"Try and walk."

"Don't leave me in the dark! I'm scared."

"I'm just getting the lantern," Addie said. "All right now, let's go back. Mother's probably worried sick."

"I don't want to go back. I've ruined everything. Everyone hates me."

Addie sighed. "If you stay here wet and shivering the rest of the night, you're going to catch a terrible cold."

"I don't know what to do," Elizabeth sobbed. She covered her muddy face with her muddy hands and crumpled into a heap. "My whole life is so miserable." She cried and cried; the sound she made was more mournful than a song dog. Addie's heart ached for her. For the first time, her cousin did not appear the least bit poised and sophisticated. She was just twelve years old, and she was confused and frightened.

Just like me, Addie thought. Gently, she placed her hand on her cousin's shoulder. "Everyone doesn't hate you. I don't hate you."

"You don't?"

Addie shook her head. "Sometimes you can be very difficult. But you're also very brave."

Elizabeth wiped her nose on her sleeve. "I am?"

"Yes, you are. You and Maudie came out west all by

yourselves. You left everything behind. Your family, your friends, your house..."

Elizabeth's mouth quivered. Was she going to burst into tears again?

"Coming to Dakota the way you did took a lot of courage," Addie persisted. "A lot more courage than most people have. Before you arrived, your mother sent us a letter. You know what she called you?"

"What?" Elizabeth stood up slowly.

"A capable, grown-up young lady."

"A capable grown-up young lady. Do you think I am?"

Addie took a deep breath. "Yes."

As the girls walked back to camp together, she was relieved to catch a glimpse of something familiar on her cousin's face. Elizabeth's awe-inspiring, fascinating, mysterious, *numinous* grin.

15 EXTRAORDINARY AND MARVELOUS

Late in the afternoon the next day, the plum pickers returned to Oak Hollow, sleepy from the bright sunshine, the rocking of the wagon, and the sweet, overpowering smell of so many red and yellow plums.

"Come on now, children. Our work isn't over yet. We need to clean and pit these plums before they spoil," Mother said. She handed the reins of the team to Pa. The children began unloading the heavy buckets and baskets from the wagon. For the first time, Elizabeth joined in without complaint.

Pa looked impressed. "You've made a good haul, Becca. Have any trouble?"

Addie held her breath. What would Mother tell him?

Mother smiled. "No trouble that didn't mend itself, Samuel."

Addie sighed with relief. That morning, before they

had left the Jim River, Mother told Maudie and Elizabeth they were welcome to stay as long as they needed to. "Rest assured we won't send you packing until we hear from my sister. I'm sure a letter will come soon."

The whole way home, Addie had sat on the back of the wagon, dangling her feet and thinking about danger and darkness and everything that had happened the night before. How impossibly black and mysterious the shadows had seemed as she searched along the Jim River! Perhaps that was what setting off on an adventure was all about— not knowing anything for absolute certain but going into the darkness anyway. In the unknown there was danger, yes. But there was something more. There was the possibility that something extraordinary and marvelous might happen, just when you least expected it.

She made up her mind. She would mail the letter to the Yankton Board of Examiners. It wasn't that she didn't want to go to school. She was just scared. And being scared no longer seemed enough reason to stay home.

"Addie, vat's de matter vit you?"

Addie started. "Take this basket for me, will you?"

"Vere you off to in such a hurry?" Tilla demanded.

"To the post office in Defiance. I'm going on horseback to mail a certain letter."

Tilla grinned. "Ven vill you be back, Miss Teacher?"

"A couple of hours. If I go bareback, I won't waste

time saddling up. If Pa or Mother asks where I am, tell them I've gone to town but I'll be back soon."

"Better take dis vit you." From her pocket, Tilla produced the smooth, white rock she had found along the road. "Keep it for good luck, Miss Teacher."

"Thanks, Tilla." Addie tucked the rock in her pocket and hurried into the barn. With trembling hands, she opened the cigar box. She found the letter from the Yankton Board of Examiners and placed it in her pocket. "Steady, Bandit," she said in a low voice as she slipped the halter over the gentle roan's head. "Giddyap!"

Confidently, she guided the horse out the back door of the barn and headed down the road toward town. With the wind in her hair, she felt as if she and Bandit were flying. Deep-down, she knew. Yes. She could leave home. She could do it all by herself.

The next morning, the sky was overcast. Addie helped George set out four wooden sawhorses beside the house. Across each pair they stretched long pieces of clean cheesecloth. In a single layer on the cloth, they arranged pitted, halved plums. Every day for the next week, after the early morning dew burned off, the plums would sit out in the sunlight to dry. Every day Burt and Lew would take turns guarding the plums from birds and other animals. Once the plums became shriveled, darkened, and leathery, they would be packed in jars with tight cork lids and stored in the root cellar.

"When winter comes," Addie said, "at least there will be plenty of stewed plums to eat."

"You're awful cheerful this morning," George complained. He was still angry that he had been left behind on the plumming expedition. "And while we're having stewed plums for breakfast, supper, and dinner, you'll be eating all kinds of fancy city food in Yankton."

Addie smiled. "I hope I will."

"Chocolate bars and licorice strips. Oyster crackers and canned peaches," George grumbled.

"I'm going to miss you, George, come October. I bet you're going to miss me, too."

Sullenly, George dumped another bucket of plums onto the cheesecloth. "You're wrong," he said in his toughest voice. "I won't miss you. Not one bit."

Addie gave George a friendly shove. He grinned.

"Somebody's coming!" Burt shouted from the soddy roof. Addie squinted. She could see a dark shape approaching on the road.

Tilla's wagon.

Addie ran, leaping barefoot over the scorched, sharp stubble. There were Tilla and Ole in the wagon seat, behind their team of bays. Addie waved. Tilla waved back. In her lap she cradled a burlap sack. Something pale blue fluttered in Ole's shirt pocket. Beside him on the wagon seat was an enormous bunch of butter-yellow black-eyed susans, ox-eyed daisies, orange butterfly milkweed, and purple blazing star—prairie flowers that had somehow managed to survive the drought.

"Kind of early in the day to be out flower picking, isn't it?" Addie called, out of breath. Ole stopped the wagon and grinned bashfully.

Tilla smiled. "My broder vas in town yesterday. I tell him to come first ting dis morning." She plucked the pale blue envelope from his pocket. "Ve brought some mail for your Iova cousins. Hop up, Addie, and ve gif you a ride."

Addie climbed up beside Tilla and took the envelope. She checked the graceful handwriting. "To Maudie and Elizabeth Nichols." The return address said, "Mrs. Edwin Nichols, Sabula, Iowa." At last, a letter from Aunt Rachel!

Ole jangled the reins, and the wagon rocked slowly forward. In the distance, Addie could see Maudie and Elizabeth standing outside the soddy. George, Lew, and Nellie May had joined Burt on the roof. Nellie jumped up and down beside her brothers, who waved their arms and shouted hello.

Addie suddenly twisted in her seat. "Say, what's that strange noise, Tilla?"

Tilla cocked her head. "Strange noise?"

"That whining. It's coming from the sack on your lap."

Tilla turned to her brother with a mocking, serious expression. "Ole, ever since ve go to de river picking plums, Addie, she is so mysterious. I tink she been to de trolls."

"Norvay trolls?" Ole asked, grinning.

"Ya, trolls like back home. I tink by dat Jim River, Addie must haf meet up vit a troll dat drag her underground. After she escape and come back, she is not de same as she used to be."

Addie laughed nervously. "Of course I'm the same."

Tilla shook her head. "You hear noises no oder ears can hear. And look at you! You sit dere vit a silly grin on your face, remembering tings nobody else knows."

"I told everyone exactly what happened that night on the Jim River, Tilla," Addie insisted. She fidgeted in embarrassment. "When I found Elizabeth in the quicksand, I simply helped her climb out."

"Dat's not vat Elizabet says."

Addie gulped. "What does she say?"

"She say you saved her life. She say you de strongest, bravest person she ever know."

Addie paused. "Well, you can't believe everything Elizabeth tells you, Tilla. She does tend to exaggerate."

"Ouch!" Tilla shifted the burlap sack in her lap.

"What have you got in there? I just saw something move."

Tilla smiled triumphantly. "Dis secret vants to come out. See here vat I brought you, Miss Teacher."

Not another Tilla present! What would it be this time?

Tilla opened the bag a crack. Two gleaming black eyes peered out.

"A puppy!" Addie exclaimed. She sat dumbfounded as a small black dog jumped out of the sack into her lap and began gnawing on the letter from Aunt Rachel.

"Papa told me and Ole to take dis one and get rid of him vit de oders before dey all starve. But ve couldn't. Ve bring him to you instead. You like him, ya? I can see dat."

Addie pulled the envelope from between the dog's needle-sharp teeth. "Well, of course I like him!"

"Good. Den it's settled! You keep him," Tilla said. Ole stopped the wagon near the barn, where Addie's brothers and sister were eagerly waiting. Addie climbed out of the wagon with the puppy.

"Hey, where'd you get that dog?" George demanded.

"Give him to me," Lew begged. "Let me hold him, Addie!"

"I got him first!" Burt grabbed and hugged the squirming black shape, but the puppy managed to wriggle free and leapt to the ground. The boys squealed as the puppy scrambled in the dirt, biting their bare toes and wrestling with their legs.

"Addie, we're going to keep him, aren't we?" George asked.

"We have to ask Pa," Addie warned. "And Mother. We'll have to ask her, too."

"Look at him!" Burt cried. "He's got such huge paws. When he grows up, I bet he's going to be as big as a buffalo."

"Come here, Buffalo!" Nellie crouched on the ground and clapped her hands together. To her delight, the puppy came running and knocked her over. The boys laughed.

"See? He's very smart," Lew said. "He already knows his name!"

Tilla, who still sat beside her brother in the wagon, elbowed Ole and motioned to Elizabeth and Maudie who were standing beside the soddy. She hissed something in Norwegian. "Addie," she said, "Ole has someting to say. He vants to say vy he came here today."

Ole cleared his throat. His face was pink. "I come here ...I come here for..."

"Go ahead, Ole," Tilla said impatiently. She gathered together the bouquet and shoved it at her brother, whose face was now bright red. "Tell her," she hissed, "you pick dese for Maudie."

"For Maudie?" Addie looked up in astonishment.

Ole nodded miserably. He did not say one word, but instead concentrated on the trembling flowers.

before they get wet."

Lightning flashed. Ole, Maudie, Tilla, and Addie struggled with the cheesecloth, while Mother and George dragged the sawhorses under cover.

Pa, who had been out in the flax field, raced into the yard after all the plums had been safely carried to the barn. "What's going on here? Why are you all standing around lallygagging like it's some kind of holiday? Can't you see there's a storm brewing? George, I thought I told you and your brothers—"

Thunder rolled. The sky seemed to quake and split. And suddenly, without warning, something marvelous and extraordinary happened.

"Whoo-peeee!" George, Lew, and Burt hollered. "It's raining!"

Rain—lovely, sweet-smelling rain! There was nothing Addie could think of that compared with the smell of those first huge drops hitting the hot dust. Instantly, the air filled with the heady scent. In seconds, the drizzle grew into a downpour. Rain trickled down her neck, behind her ears, between her toes. She tilted back her head and let the water pour down her forehead, her nose, and across her cheeks. She watched it roll off her bare arms and punch craters into the hard ground. More rain came, harder now. She opened her mouth. She had almost forgotten such delicious coolness!

"Come on, Buffalo!" the boys hollered. The puppy, who had never seen rain before in his life, bravely followed as the boys marched and splashed around the yard.

Water gurgled down the soddy roof and filled the empty cisterns. It bucked and bounced and babbled off the barn. It coursed and raced along the ground in singing, healing rivers. Nellie yodeled. She darted happily in and out among her parents and Ole and Maudie, fascinated by the ungrown-up way they carried on—all soaking wet and not frowning one bit.

"Pa?" Lew shouted, his face streaming. "Tilla gave us this dog." He held the drenched puppy high in the air so that Pa could admire Buffalo's black, glistening fur. "Can we keep him, Pa? Please?"

"A dog?" Pa said. All the worry seemed washed from his face. "A dog? Well, sure we can keep the dog. Why not? It's raining. Where's a dog going to go on a day like this?"

Lew and his brothers whooped. They waltzed with Buffalo through the puddles, tumbling together as wild and playful as puppies themselves. Nellie May twirled. And, of course, McCoggy twirled, too.

Tilla grabbed Addie's hand. Addie grabbed Elizabeth's. And the three girls spun around and around and around in a dizzy joyful circle.

LAURIE LAWLOR began creating the character of Addie while unraveling Dakota homesteading stories told by her mother and grandmother. What began as an investigation of family folklore ended in a two-year research project that ultimately took Ms. Lawlor back to South Dakota to the actual site of her great-grandparents' farm. Hundred-year-old photographs, letters, diaries, oral histories, census records, newspaper accounts, deeds, and reminiscences were all part of the material she used in *Addie Across the Prairie, Addie's Dakota Winter, Addie's Long Summer,* and *George on His Own.*

Laurie Lawlor teaches as well as writes. She lives with her husband and two children in Evanston, Illinois.